DATE DUE			

a boy called plum

BOOKS BY DARRELL A. ROLERSON

A Boy Called Plum
In Sheep's Clothing
Mr. Big Britches
A Boy and a Deer

a boy called plum

DARRELL A. ROLERSON

Illustrated by Ted Lewin

DODD, MEAD & COMPANY · NEW YORK

For my father,
who was a good storyteller—
and for Rosemary Casey,
who knows a lot about good storytelling, too

Children and feather merchants,
Listen to the birds sing!

a boy called plum

chapter one

Out over the sea the sun rose, spinning in the haze like a dandelion blazing through a web of dew. In the meadow, the bluegrass opened. The red rooster mustered himself on the sawhorse, swelling like a royal trumpeter. *"Good morning to you! Good morning to you!"* The proud cock jumped down, strutting, and tripped on his wing.

Rudyard was off in a dream of a great blue heron wading in the sea. Only the sea wasn't green; it was black. And the heron wasn't blue; it was black. At every step the heron took, from its raised foot the moon dripped silver.

Awakening quickly, with no such stretching and yawning as usual, Rudyard sat straight up on the edge of his bed and stuck both legs at once into his dirty jeans. He left his shoes where he had kicked them away until fall and hurried to the window. On

11

the shed roof the drenched trees were raining dew. Down through the green canopy of locust limbs, the pale sun came streaking like a cat.

Rudyard could hardly wait to button his shirt, he was in such a hurry. He could hear Marmy stirring in her kitchen below, and the odor of her cooking wafted up the stairs as if it were the old woman herself. Rudyard thought: Summer always begins on the day after school lets out—and so much the better when it lands on a Thursday, for that's Marmy's bake day. Chocolate-cake-with-peanut-butter-frosting day! Rudyard took another whiff and decided. Before Marmy called him for breakfast, he had just time to begin his summer.

Sitting on the open windowsill, Rudyard swung both feet over and out onto the shed. Around him on the roof the sun lay broken in beads of dew, burning like the fire in pale green emeralds. The cold beads sparkled on his feet as he stood there. He breathed deeply. The salt air misting off the sea and the fog that rolled off the warm rocks smelled like fresh mushrooms. Rudyard followed the shed roof down; he curled his toes around the edge of it and jumped; he was surprised to feel the ground so hard, so sudden beneath his tender feet—so wet—so green!

He wanted to run around the back of the barn but he walked instead, limping where the sharp stones were strewn, picking his steps like an old woman on corns. Out under Marmy's clothesline Rudyard hobbled. He hardly noticed the mackerel net Parpy had hung there, a hundred weedy feet of it that started at the barn and faded away to the orchard like wind. He paid no heed to the apple-blossom clouds, either—pink petals blowing in flurries down across the meadow and out to sea. He didn't even notice the garden where the cucumbers were just breaking ground in their brown patch at the end of the rows. He was too busy concentrating on his feet, dancing on his toes through the pricker bushes. He was thankful when he hit the lawn again. The wet green grass was soft beneath his feet and the dandelions were thick as stars.

Out in front of the barn the tower stood. It was reared against the sky; it was stern against the sea; braced like an old sea captain on crutches. Rudyard grabbed the ladder and started up, climbing where the wind blew. His yellow hair flared like a torch. As he climbed, the tower swayed, but Rudyard wasn't afraid that it would crumble. Parpy himself had built the tower, longer ago than Rudyard could remember. It had stood through a dozen hurricanes, and not till last fall had the wind blown strong enough to rip away its roof and buckle its shins. Even now, Parpy said, the tower was as strong as if she'd been built on the church. Parpy had spent his life around boats, and so he always referred to the tower as "she." He'd built her for water, originally, but now that she was broke, he was too old to do anything but lug his water from the spring. As soon as Rudyard was old enough, the first thing he'd do for Parpy was mend the tower, though Parpy never complained. One good thing about the spring, Parpy always said, was the eel that lived there of its own accord, and the frog. Parpy had thought of moving the frog to Marmy's rain barrel, so it would clean up the larvae the mosquitoes laid there in her wash water. But, though one good eel was enough to keep the spring water purified, Parpy wasn't sure the frog would be happy in a rain barrel.

On this first day of summer, Rudyard reached the top of the tower in record time. He climbed up onto the narrow ledge, where he crouched, as if on a porch before some small house. But, without any roof, it looked more like some big tub—one that would hold a lot more than three men. Rudyard had often thought how it would be if he were blown away to sea in it. He could sail to Africa and see a gorilla and bring back rare spices for Marmy's cooking.

Rudyard looked around. On the barn, the black-horse weather vane galloped, its iron mane blazing in the wind; above the house the blue smoke poured from Marmy's chimney as if the whole sky were coming right from her kitchen. The dew steaming off the tops of the locust trees drew Rudyard's breath thin with the smell of it. He closed his eyes and savored it, as he savored the sweet cinnamon rolls he stole from Marmy's pantry and ate while they were still hot. Rudyard lingered—but then he remembered that he really didn't have a moment to spare and he ducked in through the little door.

Rudyard stood up on his toes and stretched and rested his chin on the tower's rim. He closed his eyes and filled himself with the wind, breathing in till he was almost bursting. He popped open his eyes; his breath came fizzling in a sigh, he let himself go like a balloon.

Out over the trees and out over the sea was Rudyard when he was in the tower—out over the meadow. He could see forever. Any way he faced in the tower, he could trace the horizon—and turning around in the tower, he could see his whole world.

Looking east, Rudyard could see the road to Gooseberry Nubble; west was where his feet had beaten a path toward the "crick"; north and south the island widened into woods, and that accounted for the trees. There was, however, no accounting for the sea. It went forever, around and around.

If it hadn't been for that big stand of hackmatacks, and a few other trees, Rudyard could have seen where the crick emptied into the sea. Besides there being no school, that was the best thing he could think about summer: Come Saturday night, Marmy didn't make him take a bath. Whenever he felt like it, he just went swimming. Beyond the crick, ravens with slick black wings were smoothing out the sky, and Rudyard could see the little fish crows drawing circles over Bounty Cove where Parpy kept the *Patient Lucy*, calked and primed and standing by for the mackerel run. Parpy said they'd run today, for sure. He'd predicted so the night before, when the lightning bugs were blinking in the meadow—blinking and blinking, bright as the moon on a phosphorescent sea. The one that blinked in Parpy's hair was the one that Rudyard caught and lugged upstairs to the dark garret where he slept.

Rudyard moved his chin along the rim of the tower and changed his view. Up and down his world was blue, and Rudyard saw it through a haze, as in a crystal ball. The roofs in the white dew out over Gooseberry Nubble shone like periwinkles in a tidal pool, and he saw gay flower gardens flaring into bloom around gray houses the color of fog and steppingstones. There were nineteen houses to be exact, not counting the little fish shacks. The houses stood with long faces, reflecting in their windows the shadows of the sea, as if they were scowling—at the sea,

15

perhaps, or at the howling wind that sometimes rattled the windows from their frames and ripped the shingles from their roofs, and now and then sent a live brick flying from a chimney.

Digging his hands deep into his pockets, Rudyard stood up on his toes as if his feet, free of his shoes this morning, were brand new. This way he got a better view. Beside the wharf where the village was centered, he could see the mailboat, waiting for her daily run to Sabathday. It was to the wharf that Rudyard went to lug home a package, now and then, when Marmy ordered something from the catalogue. That roof over there was Trim's store; over there, the church; and down a way was the school, where all the erasers lay pounded in a row and Rudyard's slate was spit-clean.

Of all the roofs that Rudyard could see, the one that interested him most was where Everard lived. Everard was his cousin. Everard had a sister, though Rudyard hesitated to call *her* his cousin. He hid from Thankful. She never thought to look for him in the tower. Or, Rudyard smiled with satisfaction, she was too afraid to climb that high. If she wanted anything it was only to plague him, anyway.

Besides being a cousin, Everard was also Rudyard's best friend, though Aunt Lucy—*that* was Everard's mother—hadn't better catch them up to any of their shenanigans. If it weren't for Aunt Lucy, Rudyard would have a friend to share the summer, but he knew he would be lucky if he saw Everard again before the fall. Aunt Lucy would see to that. She didn't want *her* son hanging around with the likes of Rudyard. She didn't want Rudyard feeding his ideas into Everard's head—"contaminating Everard's mind," Aunt Lucy said. So she would send Everard lobstering every day, with his father—every day except Sunday. The only way Rudyard would get to see Everard was if they both went to Sunday School, which was just the way Aunt Lucy had planned. Rudyard was the only boy in town who didn't go to Sunday School, she said. Aunt Lucy was into predictions, too. "Why," she said, "the next thing you know that boy will take to gambling!" And it was true; Rudyard already had a lucky rock. And though he'd give his lucky rock to see Everard, right now or come Sunday, he was mighty grateful that Marmy didn't make him go to Sunday School.

Just then Rudyard heard the motor being choked on Uncle Harvey's lobster boat. What a way for summer to begin—with Everard and Uncle Harvey spending the whole day hauling the traps they had set completely around the island. When they got home it would be night, and too late for Rudyard and Everard to see each other, because neither of them would pass through the cemetery woods alone after it got dark. Just looking at those woods gave Rudyard the chills. During the day when he went that way, he ran.

Rudyard lowered his eyes. Over there, at the end of the meadow—at the edge of the alder swamp where the digging was easy—he had helped bury his pets. When he died, *that's* where he wanted to go, with the cat and the horse and sixteen birds. Under *no* condition did he want to be buried in the woods. Aunt Lucy said if you walked into those woods at night and stomped your feet around, the whole ground would be hollow. That's what Aunt Lucy said was hell. It was almost like Aunt Lucy herself

17

had put it there, to keep the boys apart.

Uncle Harvey revved the engine on his lobster boat and gathered speed. Just when Rudyard knew the boat would appear, out beyond the chimney tops, he turned. He looked away, suddenly reluctant to begin his summer. He sent his mind across the bay. Often he had thought that walking around the shore forever would never get him to the mainland. Over in Sabathday the mountains rolled up out of the sea like dinosaurs. Since Rudyard had never been to Sabathday, he thought of it simply as "Away," as everyone else on the island did. He had spent a lot of time considering all the things that he might find there—all the *places*! Some of them were on the map, and some of them—like the island—weren't. Rudyard was glad of that. It left *him* places to discover.

The rush of wings above his head attracted his attention, and when he looked up he saw a bird, as if it had been summoned

from his dream. It was as big as a boy, with wings spread wider than arms. If Rudyard had reached out a moment sooner he could have touched it. He just stood fixed and watched the great bird drifting down the sky, like a mobile of hollow bones balanced full of feathers. He watched until the red sun scorched his eyes. And when the bird was gone, Rudyard felt as if he could sing, or jump up and down, or do most anything.

Marmy said, for Heaven's sake, not to get the notion *he* could fly. But Rudyard could do his flying right in his head. He simply opened himself to the wind. He let his mind soar up, where the swallows soared—up where their merry singing sounded like wingtips squeaking against the sky. Or he swooped down, where the meadow grew in bright patches; around and around he flew above the blossoms.

But it wouldn't be any fun being a bird if he had to contend with a cat. Just then Hey-Diddle-Diddle, the Cat, brought Rudyard back to his senses. He could see her now, over in the barn, stretching herself awake in the window where the calico sun was just spilling across the sill. How fat was the cat now that she was full of kittens!

Dingbat crawled out from under the porch, driven out, no doubt, by his fleas. And he looked straight up into the tower, caught Rudyard's eye, and winked . . . as bird dogs do. And right then Rudyard knew that his summer had begun.

Parpy whirled out of the barn like a squall driven by the wind, his grizzly beard a week old and his sleeves rolled up clean to his elbows. In his hands was a bowl of milk, and there beside him, bucking all the way, was Buttercups. Marmy met them at

19

the door and shooed the goat with her apron. "Scat!" she said. "Get away!"

And Buttercups went, while Hey-Diddle-Diddle, the Cat, streaked into the kitchen between Parpy's feet. Marmy pulled the screen door shut. She hollered up through the screen, up through the locust green.

"Ruud-yard.

"Come, Plum," she called.

"Breakfast.

"*Yoooo-hoooo!*"

-2-

Marmy had risen with the sun to stoke the fire and poke the stove full of biscuit wood, to fiddle with the dampers and the drafts. Now that the oven was up to five hundred, the kitchen was hot, and Marmy was obliged to open the parlor and serve breakfast on the round oak table which was usually spread only for feasts.

One corner of the parlor was Parpy's. There were his easy chair and a radio so big that the people he listened to could almost have stood inside it. Mostly Parpy listened to hear what the weather would be, though he usually knew better—rain was never far away on the island. Parpy wasn't much interested in the other news; the biggest advantage of having a radio, he was apt to say, was being able to turn it off. Aunt Lucy kept him tuned in to what was happening on the island; as for the news from Away, he read *The Republican Journal*, though mostly, he said, *that* was good just to start the fire with or for Marmy to put down when she washed the floor.

Sometimes Parpy told Rudyard stories of ghosts and hermits, and special ones about a crotch-eye watching in a tree, and a jealous pirate whose wife was so beautiful he cut off her head and took it to sea. And there were stories of places that were too far away to be on any map—places with castles and royal palaces and cathedrals. Even if Parpy repeated a story, Rudyard always listened as if hearing it new, for Parpy told it as if for the first time—surprising himself, even; sometimes he changed the end.

Everybody around said that Parpy was the best storyteller in the world. So he must be, Rudyard figured, and he was pleased to call his grandfather Parpy, though most people on the island called him Captain. Marmy blushed when she called him John.

Another corner of the parlor was Marmy's. There was her rocking chair, over it a shawl that she had knitted, using odd bits of yarn which she had gathered like a bird; there was a stool to rest her feet; and another stool with a swivel seat where Marmy sometimes sat and played the organ and sang "Sweet Adeline." Rudyard had to get down under the organ and pump, because Marmy's poor corns, she said, were in no condition. But she could sing like a bird, and from beneath the organ Rudyard could look up and see her throat warble on the high parts. Sometimes the spirit would sting him, and he would break out singing. And Parpy, too! Once when Parpy had sampled a new batch of his rhubarb wine he showed Rudyard how to dance the hybiddy-woodchuck, while Marmy played and sang, "Oh Johnny! Oh Johnny! Oh!" When Parpy was finished, Marmy laughed and said that he was full of *more gristle*! But when Rudyard asked him to do it again, Parpy said at eighty-one it's a wonder a man can stiver and go, let alone be doing the hy-biddy-woodchuck.

Marmy was fiddling with the damper on the stove when Rudyard came down from the tower and into the kitchen. He washed at the iron sink with spring water he ladled from the bucket and splashed across his face. It was so cold it made his fingers ache. He rose with a gasp, as he often did after plunging in the sea, but instead of salt things drying in the sun, he smelled the sweet things Marmy was baking in her oven. He wiped his face and hurried to the parlor, raring to begin.

The braids in Marmy's homemade rug felt good beneath his feet, and Rudyard dug in his toes. Parpy was already at the table, pleased as could be, this morning, as he sat there leaning on his elbow. Marmy thought it *might* not be etiquette. Aunt Lucy said it *definitely* wasn't good etiquette to eat with your elbows on the table. But Parpy did it anyway, and his elbow was torn right out of his sleeve. One thumb was hooked into his green suspenders, as if that part of him was posing for a sea captain. Parpy's shoulder bones poked through his shirt like sticks. On the first day of summer he had a twinkle in his eyes. "Haul up a chair, Plum."

But Rudyard had something else on his mind. He walked straight to Marmy's china closet. There, locked behind the glass, Marmy kept a little jug that had come all the way from China. On it was a great blue heron. The bird flew like paint swept in strokes across the china-blue sky.

"I saw a crane today," Rudyard said, for Parpy liked great blue herons, too, and that was what he called them.

"I presume they're waiting for the mackerel to run, too," Parpy said, "just like the rest of us."

"Is *that* what they eat?" Rudyard asked. He thought they lived on frogs and minnows.

"When they can get it," Parpy said, "that's what they like better than anything."

Rudyard had to think about that. "I like chocolate cake with peanut butter frosting better than anything—" he said, "when I can get it." He added the last part for Marmy's benefit, for he could smell her coming. She was like an incense whose fragrance moves with the air.

Rudyard hauled up a chair and sat down and stuck his toes around a rung. He put his elbow on the table, too. Marmy heard what he had said and took his teasing good naturedly.

"What kind of a bird was that?" she asked.

"A crane," Rudyard said, and then, because it was the kind of thing to tell Marmy, he added, "I had a dream about one last night."

"You dreamed about one, *too!*" Marmy said.

"*Mmm-hmmm*," Rudyard said. "A black one."

"A *black* one!" Marmy exclaimed. "It sounds to me like you'd better be concerned with something besides chocolate cake with peanut butter frosting. Sounds to *me* like you've seen an omen." In one hand Marmy delivered the porridge, steaming under goat's milk and sweetened with honey, and in the other, a kettle full of applesauce. Rudyard could smell hot cinnamon.

He bolstered himself up on both elbows, now. "What's an

23

omen?" he asked.

"Land sakes, Plum. I thought you knew all about omens," Marmy said. "An omen is a sign that something's soon to happen."

"Something *bad?*" Rudyard asked—for coming from Marmy, it sounded horrible.

Parpy had seen Rudyard's eyes bug out. "Now, now," he said. "Let's not scare the boy."

But Rudyard swallowed. "I ain't scairt," he asserted.

Marmy shook her head. "I'm just telling him for his own good. Some birds are ill omens," she said, and off she took again for the kitchen. Marmy gripped Rudyard's shoulder as she passed, as if to solace him for the bad news and at the same time ease up a little on her corns—just enough to get her started.

When she had gone, Rudyard turned to Parpy. "What about herons for birds? What kind of omens are they? Ill ones?"

Parpy shook his head. "I ain't so familiar with omens myself," he said.

Rudyard insisted. "But if they *was* ill omens . . ."

"You can't tell until it happens," Parpy said.

"Till *what* happens!"

"Whatever the omen meant was supposed to happen," Parpy said. "Let's not jump to conclusions."

"You mean I have to wait?"

"*Aa-yup,*" Parpy said. "It kind of looks that way. 'Less you take up with a gypsy. They tell fortunes, you know."

Rudyard reminded him, "Aunt Lucy predicts."

"There's a difference," Parpy said.

"There sure *is* a difference," Marmy agreed, as she returned, wincing, on her corns. She brought her men a platterful of brown biscuits vibrating in the sun that shone through the window, and a pot of black tea. "Speaking of ill omens," Marmy said, all set to pick up where she left off, "when I was a girl, *we* had filly-loo-birds. Now you're lucky if you don't run into one of them."

"Tell me about *them*!" Rudyard said.

"*Narh!*" Marmy replied, "I know darn well you don't want to hear about filly-loo-birds," when she knew darn well he did.

"Oh-yes-I-do!" Rudyard said.

"Well—" Marmy looked at him a little gravely. "If you really want to know—" she said.

"I do."

"When I was a girl, if a filly-loo-bird flew down your chimney it meant you was good as dead."

"You mean . . ." Rudyard gulped. "Tell me some more!"

But just then Parpy gave Marmy one of his looks that was as good as a nudge. Marmy rolled her eyes up into her head. "There's some things solemn to us all," she said. And Rudyard knew not to coax any more.

Marmy pulled up a chair and settled down. Because her hair was like thistledown, the wind took it everywhere, so even in the house she kept her head wrapped in a bandanna. The bandanna reminded Rudyard of a picture he had seen in his geography book, so that Marmy looked to him like someone from Away.

"Heave to," Parpy said, and Rudyard began.

Marmy sat with her great freckled arms folded in her lap. She looked askance at Rudyard's elbow, and looked again, but then she noticed Parpy's elbow, and so she bowed her head over her porridge and she began, too, thinking, probably, "What would Aunt Lucy say?"

Rudyard thought of birds of ill omen as he ate; he thought of eagles and ospreys and great blue herons; and of a picture Marmy had, hanging on the wall, of pink flamingoes wading in a swamp in Florida. He couldn't get his mind on breakfast *this* morning. Out of the corner of one eye he saw Hey-Diddle-Diddle angling her tail like a worm, as she listened to the birds singing in the locust tree and on the lawn. It was hard to tell what the cat was thinking as she lay sprawled on the windowsill. Her bulk was wedged in between pots of red begonias, which she was wary not to spill, lest Marmy whack her with the broom. She lay with her black eye open; her green eye was cast against the sun that shone like autumn in her fur and on her cocked orange ear. She watched with cat-detachment as breakfast was being eaten—until it was time to pour some milk, and then she licked her yellow whiskers and began to purr.

Parpy was finished first, except for his tea. "Buttercups came home with red hoofs," he said, which meant that in the meadow the wild strawberries were ripe.

"Holy-je-hossifats!" Marmy said. "They *ain't!*"

But Parpy assured her that they were. "After all," he said, "it's the first day of summer."

"Then we shall have to get a wiggle on," Marmy said—indicating Rudyard. "And you will have to help me, Plum."

Rudyard slumped down in his chair as if already his omen had come true.

"Just fetch me some jam jars up from the cellar," she said. "An armful will be a plenty. Then you can run along." Marmy fluttered her fingers.

Parpy reminded them, "And don't forget. Today's the day the mackerel should run." What he meant was, better fetch some jars up for the canning of them, too.

"Gawdfrediamonds!" Marmy lamented for the sake of it. "It's that time of year again. If it ain't six of one thing, it's half a dozen of the other."

Rudyard left his tea immediately. If *all* he had to do was lug a few jars . . . he went through the parlor door and straight across the kitchen and into the pantry. He stooped and tugged at the rope handle sticking out of the floor. The cellar door opened before him. Rudyard had started down when all the mouth-watering odors in the world anchored him, right there on the first rung of the ladder. He looked around at the pantry, at the brown eggs and ripe bananas ready to be made into bread, at the hot custard pie with burnt flowers of nutmeg bursting on its top. He heard himself thinking, "Thursday is bake day! Chocolate-cake-with-peanut-butter-frosting day . . ."

But he heard Marmy coming and turned away, afraid she might suspect him. As he backed down the ladder he saw a sour cream pie and molasses cookies—spread to cool on the counter—staring him in the eye! Cookies as big as biscuits! Rudyard knew they were soft as cake inside . . . and sweet! As he disappeared down the hatch, his nose caught the last lingering whiff, so he could hardly wait until he came back up again.

No sooner was Rudyard's head below the floor than the odor of the cellar engulfed him. He could smell the spice and vinegar, the dill in the pickles, and the sour mold in the old pumpkin, stored since fall, which was just beginning to rot. The essence of another season was always locked in the cellar—the musk of spring was in the soil, and the fruit of fall was in the bins, where a few fragrant apples with wrinkled skins lay waiting to be made into pies.

The last step down was a big one. The oak leaves Parpy used to store the apples in were rotting now, scraped from the bins. Rudyard could feel them beneath his feet, where the worms were busy twelve months a year spinning them into new soil—*rich* soil that would never see the sun, unless Marmy had him lug some up to put new life into one of her red begonias. The wet leaves were under Rudyard's feet, and between his toes where he could still feel the chair rung. He stared into the dark, waiting for his eyes to adjust. Parpy had opened the vent to dry the cellar out so the sills that held the house up wouldn't rot. Rudyard could hear the chickens squabbling over sowbugs and centipedes out beneath the porch.

Through the open vent the daylight came like cobwebs streaming through the night. And gray slugs crept, dragging the day behind them in snotty trails left glimmering . . . up and down the wet, stone walls and all around the jars of preserves . . . around the stewed crabapples and mincemeat and chokecherry jelly. And *twice* around Marmy's green tomato relish. Rudyard couldn't think of anything good to say about a slug. Parpy said he couldn't, either. Sowbugs and centipedes were okay for hens; and the worms were good for gardens; they could even turn *him* into new soil if he stood there long enough. Rudyard jumped. But a *slug*!

Rudyard picked out the smallest jars for wild strawberry jam, and took as many as he could, gathering them under his arms. He almost put a kink in his leg getting up the ladder. Marmy was in the pantry, peeking down, waiting for him so she could help. He passed the jars up to her, one at a time, and counted . . . fourteen.

"That's enough, Plum," she said.

But when Rudyard started up the rest of the way, Marmy stopped him. "Oh, dear," she said. "Don't forget the Mason jars. Quart ones for the mackerel."

It was like forgetting to say "May I?" Rudyard had to go all the way back down. He took the big jars under his arms and struggled up the ladder and passed them one at a time across the pantry floor. But he could only carry five at once, and not until he'd made six trips was Marmy satisfied. Then she said again, "That's enough, Plum."

Rudyard hustled up out of the cellar and banged the hatch door, eager to be done. But on second thought, "I'll take care of them," he said, and was very careful not to let Marmy see him looking at the molasses cookies.

"Oh, will you, Plum?" Marmy was pleased. She glanced down at the jars. "If you would just put them in the sink for me. It hurts for me to bend." And off she went, wincing, to her kitchen, where she took the crank and started shaking down the ashes in the stove.

Rudyard hurried with the jars, taking time to scan the cookies. He poked one to see how soft they were. His light fingers were itching. He counted out a fistful to fit in his pocket. He could have put a fistful in his other pocket, too, except it was so full of stuff. He whistled a little monotone as he worked. If he was quiet in her pantry, Marmy would suspect him.

Rudyard heard the kitchen floor creak. He crammed a cookie into his mouth—a *big* one! He crammed until his face was bursting. He hurried out looking as if he had the mumps.

Marmy was on her way to the pantry, wiping out a berry pail. "Today you can shift for yourselves," she was saying. "I won't be home in time for dinner. There'll be strawberry shortcake for supper, though."

"*Um*!" Rudyard said, and hurried out the door.

-3-

Rudyard stopped running at the end of the meadow. His mouth was full of half-chewed cookie and he was blowing through his nose like a racehorse. He tumbled down in the animal cemetery—with the horse and the cat and sixteen birds. He grabbed Dingbat by a hind leg and dragged the dog down, too, in the redtop and timothy. Dingbat's long tongue was hanging out like a tongue in an old shoe. He shook himself loose and limped up, pointing at a bee. Aunt Lucy always told Rudyard that *he* should never point! But she had no objections to Dingbat who pointed with a paw, at this and that, as if he were conducting a tour.

Rudyard broke the cookies out of his pocket and fed a few crumbs to Dingbat, who stopped panting long enough to beg for more. Marmy called the dog Dingbat when she wanted him, but when she didn't she called him a son of a black and tan and told him to *git*! Rudyard could see a lot of black and tan in Dingbat, especially around his long nose.

Just then Buttercups came galloping. Her ears were in a gale and her long, white goatee was streaming from her chin. She was harder to get away from than Everard's sister. She stood dangling her wattles over Rudyard, sniffing. But the cookies were gone. Rudyard offered her some nice toes, which he wiggled to make them more enticing. They looked parboiled from the dew. Buttercups took one whiff of them, scoffed, and went off grazing in the columbine and sweet red clover.

Dingbat pointed at a black butterfly with pollen on its tail the color of gold. It almost landed on Dingbat's nose, but he barked. The butterfly settled on the down of a devil's paintbrush, until Dingbat went over and poked at it. Then the butterfly winged against the sun, fluttering like Marmy's fingers over piecrust.

Rudyard knelt and picked a handful of the paintbrushes. He chose a red one and laid it on a yellow stone. That one was for Patient Lucy. Patient Lucy had been a horse, though now that she was dead Parpy had put her name to good use on his dory. The grass was always greenest over Patient Lucy's grave. Rudyard wondered if it wasn't because she'd eaten so much of it when she was alive.

The next grave was marked by a clay flower pot, turned upside-down. Rudyard stuck a yellow paintbrush into the pot's drain hole. That was for Pandora, Marmy's tomcat that stayed wild for five years, and then came home one day to die.

All the other graves in the cemetery were for birds, that Rud-

31

yard and Marmy had found, so it was really heaven there for Pandora. Rudyard chose one paintbrush after another—a red and a yellow and a red and a red and a red. It was his favorite color. He sat back and wound the last red paintbrush between his toes, surveying the graves. Parpy said it was getting to be like a national cemetery.

Rudyard looked up over the knoll, just in time to see Everard's sister coming over the hill, with her ugly mug looking all four ways for him. With the flower between his toes, Rudyard bounded away into the alder swamp.

Catkins dangled from the limbs like caterpillars waiting for their wings as Rudyard hurried past them, down the black, packed path that was hard as leather beneath his feet. He kicked a skunk cabbage as he went, and hurried away from the stink, up past the jack-in-the-pulpits. Buttercups followed him, stopping for a treat of pussy willows that had gone to seed.

Rudyard raced Dingbat up out of the swamp, until they came beneath the hackmatack trees. Rudyard dropped down on his knees in the moss and the soft brown patches of wood grass. Since the tide was low, anyway, and he couldn't go swimming in the crick yet, there wasn't any hurry. There was only one thing left to do—hunt crabs. Unless he wanted to skip rocks until his arm was lame.

He stretched out under the trees and looked up at the sky that was hurrying by in eight shades of blue. Dingbat pointed at a chickadee that was drinking rain from the bright orange carapace of a crab. The chickadee flew, and Dingbat turned around three times and stretched out, too, and Buttercups went off grazing in the fiddleheads. Rudyard closed his eyes. Inside the island he could feel the sea, beating like the blood in his own veins. He sighed and began to dream.

It didn't seem possible that school was out—that here it was Thursday. And here *he* was! Not that he was *sorry* it was summer; it was only the first day, and he had waited so long to put away his shoes; but he wiggled his toes and felt sorry he didn't have a friend to throw rocks with and swim. He fluttered his eyes and the bright blue sky darted in and out of his brain. "Omen," he said.

"*O*-men," he repeated, as if after a prayer, while he was wondering: What did it mean? A good omen might mean his parents were coming home. If his father came he'd have someone to go lobstering with—the way Everard did. Marmy said for him not to count on it. His father, she said, was like a tomcat: *In*dependent. Parpy said he might be independent, but even a tomcat comes home to die.

If his father *did* come home, his mother would come, too. For how long had they been gone, now? Ever since Rudyard could remember. The only thing that Rudyard knew about his parents was that Aunt Lucy hadn't liked them any more than she liked him. She said, in fact, that he was a big discrepancy in their relationship—whatever *that* meant. He knew not to ask Aunt Lucy. He tried to get Marmy and Parpy to tell him. But try as he would, whenever it came to his mother and father, he couldn't get Marmy and Parpy to say much—as if they were afraid of saying something big that Rudyard would only complicate with questions. He liked to ask. Not that he cared much, except he won-

33

dered, now and then, where they were. Marmy said, oh, of course, they were off somewhere gallivanting, and Rudyard thought that it was true—probably in Rome, or Spain, or a hundred other places that he knew. Perhaps they had even become gypsies! He couldn't blame them for *that*!

In fact, Rudyard's father had come from Away to begin with, so he could have been a gypsy all the time. But Rudyard's mother had been born right on the island. Parpy explained it was a weakness among the people in his family that they always loved someone from Away, though, he had to admit, Marmy had panned out pretty well—and *she* was from Away. But it *could* be a problem, breaking in someone from Away, Parpy said, and gave Aunt Lucy as an example.

When he grew up, Rudyard thought, what was the sense in getting married anyway—if all he had to choose from was Everard's ugly sister? What he wanted to be more than anything was a sea captain—to sail the seven seas and be his own master—to be accountable to no one, except the wind, and to be able, even, to work that so it would take him any place in the world. Parpy said it was okay to dream, but there weren't any more sea captains in this day, and whoever wanted to be one had been born too late. Rudyard thought if he couldn't be a sea captain, at least he could live on a houseboat and grow watermelons on deck; or maybe . . . just *may-be*, Rudyard thought, he could be a gypsy.

"A *Gypsy*!" he said.

He was surprised he hadn't thought of it before. Then he wouldn't have to wait to find out what his omen meant. If he were a gypsy he would know. He jumped up and set off down the path—hopping, sometimes, like a rabbit, and chanting to the trees, "A gypsy! A gypsy!"

Buttercups discovered the May apples in bloom and ate some, and helped herself to bugbane, too, and a dogtooth violet. She sniffed a purple trillium, but turned her nose up at that and ran. Rudyard was waiting for her behind a tree. When she caught up to him, he jumped out—"A *gyp*-seee!"

He and Buttercups and Dingbat moseyed on their way, stopping once to chip a little pitch gum off a tree. It tasted like the forest smelled, and as soon as Rudyard swallowed it he stopped again to pick a bright red berry of wintergreen to freshen his mouth.

It was low tide when they reached the crick. The brown flats glistened through the trees and the warm breeze smelled like juniper on Buttercups' breath. At the top of the bank, Rudyard picked a bay leaf to nibble on his way. He curled his toes into the cool clay to keep from slipping. The bay leaf burned his tongue as Rudyard imagined rum would. It made him think about the time that Parpy treated him to a swig of rhubarb wine, and he wondered, what would Aunt Lucy say? Rudyard lurched down the bank, half drunk by the time he got to the bottom. Aunt Lucy would have scolded him for such an act.

But Rudyard sobered up in record time when he saw that Dingbat was pointing, and he froze. Not ten feet away, in the sallow shadows by the eelgrass, a heron stood . . . splendid in its own reflection. At first Rudyard thought that it was *two*, stalking the minnows that were stranded there in a tidal pool. He breathed one word, "Omen." The great bird rose into the air with the sun bursting in its wings.

Rudyard broke and Dingbat started barking. Rudyard ran along the shore's granite rim where the salt rime was drying on the rocks and a pink vein of quartz rippled like fat off a lean hog. Buttercups was bouncing after him. A seagull saw them coming and flew away screaming to the sky, "*Whyyyy? Whyyyy? Whyyyy?*" Sandpipers picking fleas from the rotting seaweed fled. Rudyard shook his head and ran, leaping, surefooted as his goat.

At the end of the beach, where the big woods came down to the sea, the heron disappeared above the trees. Rudyard leaped over the rotting seaweed and scrambled up the bank after it. The wild pear was flung in the wind like a white door blossoming before him in the wild, black tangle. The trees grew so thick the sun could only bounce from limb to limb like the squirrels that never touched the ground. He crashed through. He dodged one tree and faced another, and dodged that one, too—dancing, this way and that, as he did when he met Aunt Lucy in the door of Trim's store, and neither of them knew which way to go.

Suddenly, Rudyard came to his senses. If he didn't expect to *catch* the bird, he didn't know *why* he was chasing it. And oh, his feet were *throbbing*! He sat down on a rock and grabbed them in both hands. One was bleeding.

A blackbird perched in a tree and screamed at him, "*Seee? Seee?*"

-4-

Rudyard's blood dried on the rock in splotches like clot-red lichens. Maybe he should soak his feet in the sea, he thought, like

Marmy did her corns when he lugged the water for her. Marmy said salt water was good for anything that ailed feet.

What would Marmy say about his seeing two herons in *one* day? If he saw two a day all summer, then what would Marmy say it meant? Rudyard raised his head to the trees. They grew so thick they hardly had room to stand, and no room to fall when they were dead. The gray-green moss among their limbs was snagged as if a procession of sea hags had passed through, wrapped in rags of mist. Rudyard hunkered down and glanced in back of him, out of the corners of his eyes. He didn't remember ever having been in *this* neck of the woods before. He forced his attention back to his toe. After awhile it stopped bleeding, so he spit on it and rubbed it in.

He climbed up on the rock and looked around. He imagined bobcats in every tree, hankering for the sweet marrow in his bones, but he tamed them all and took them home—to Marmy's surprise; she made him sleep with them in the barn!

But he soon grew tired of that game. He listened for the sea, to find which way he should go. But above him in the trees the limbs and leaves washed together like surf. Rudyard stared up into the writhing green, and down again at his feet; he wiggled his cut toe, though he wasn't *really* thinking about it. What was it Marmy had said about filly-loo-birds?

Rudyard turned slowly, facing the direction from which he'd come. But there wasn't any path there . . . or *anywhere*. He turned all the way around. In the trees he could hear the wind sobbing as through a muffled fist, but the air he breathed was pale and thin and did not stir. Could he have run clear into the cemetery woods? Rudyard felt more than the presence of trees. And just then a current riled the woods and whisked him a dead leaf—what more proof did he need?—whisked the leaf right past his nose and through the shadows gathered in the trees. In the breeze's wake, the half-fallen trees around him creaked and groaned.

He was only stalling for the time it took to gather his wits. "Cranes ain't filly-loo-birds," he said, speaking half to himself and half to the trees. "And besides—one didn't fly down *my* chimney!" But he didn't sound too convinced.

When Rudyard looked again at his cut toe, he saw that he was standing in a feeding ground for crows. The rock was covered with bones, and the sharp, broken shells of clams, turned creeping green. Urchins with quills balled up like tiny porcupines barricaded his feet, and some without quills lay strewn about like hollow sockets, as if their eyes had been plucked out. Somewhere in the trees the crows were chuckling over their sacrifices, mocking him. Buttercups looked up, and raised her ears as if she had caught a spook in them . . . straight up, as if they were meters for Rudyard's fear. And where was Dingbat now that *he* was needed?

Rudyard leaped down from the rock and began to run, zigzagging through the mossy graveyard of trees. The sharp, dry twigs caught and held him like angry talons, while spider webs broke like nerves across his face. He ran as if a swarm of bees were after him—straight toward the sea. He looked for it to sparkle through the trees, but the harder he ran the more it seemed he was running in circles. He fell down on his knees and looked up. All he wanted was to see the sky, but all he saw was brush and dead limbs hanging over him and gray moss clinging on trunks like rags rotting on corpses. And the crows were dickering: "Who will give a

38

black feather for *his* hide?" Sickening fear turned sour in his throat.

Somewhere in the woods his dog was barking. Rudyard crashed through the brush in that direction. Saucers of green light spilled down like the sun shining through a thunderhead. *Good old Dingbat!* Rudyard stumbled to the clearing. *The sky!* He wanted to run right out beneath it; he wanted to wave his hands and cry, "Here I am! Here I am!" But the raspberry bushes kept him back with little thorns like teeth grinning at his naked feet.

All around him, bleaching in the sun, piles of dried brush were stacked where someone had been cutting wood. Rudyard sighed with relief. He had been here before. He took his stance in the sun, looking up at the one black spruce that stood in the clearing. Its great limbs were raised to the sky like a bandleader about to strike up the universe. Yellow blades of sun sliced through it, flashing sharp across Rudyard's eyes. He shielded them with his hand, anxious to see why Dingbat was whimpering and pointing. Rudyard's eyes opened wide and his heart perked like Dingbat's ears. High up in the boughs the heron stood, as stiff and gray as a clay model.

Dingbat pawed the ground like a bull, thundering in his throat. *"Dingbat!"* Rudyard commanded, as he had heard Parpy do. The dog was still. But the lone gray sentinel flew back against the sky, screaming.

Rudyard forgot that he was lost. He forgot about his feet. He forgot about ill omens, even. All he knew was the flood of wings that swept the sky, climbing high in crests and plunging. Rudyard squeezed his chest in tight, holding it with both his hands as if it

39

were a kite that he was flying. And bending his knees he dipped and dived and soared, too, feeling such giddy height deep in the pit of his stomach that it put goosebumps on his spine. Rudyard opened his mouth to the sky and laughed, he felt so good! He expected the bird to drift out over the trees and disappear, but it swept around the wind-whipped crown of the tree, around and around, rasping as if it were caught in a whirlwind. At first Rudyard thought that maybe it was.

Rudyard looked up so straight he almost fell over backward when he saw the nest. He staggered and stood in awe. His mouth was full of wonder. Without looking down he parted the bushes one at a time and waded through, till the nest above him was a black silhouette of sticks bundled against the sun. The tree tapered to the sky like a mast for the island to sail by—it must be as high, even, as the tower! If only there was a ladder to the top . . . his eyes fell through the tree a hundred feet before they started up again, one stout limb at a time . . . all he had to do was reach the first!

Rudyard never gave it a second thought. He spread his small arms wide across the pitchy trunk, then patted it as if it were a horse he meant to mount. It was a long, sticky way to shinny. Once Rudyard thought he might let go and fall back into the bushes and fill his whole body with thorns. And he saw himself at the bottom of the tree looking like a pincushion. What if he got lockjaw? That was his first concern, lockjaw being the *worst* thing anybody can get! And though it usually comes from stepping on rusty nails, Aunt Lucy said for sure, it can come from other things.

That was all the boost he needed. The next thing Rudyard knew, he was hauling himself up onto the first limb. There he sat, with both legs dangling; he paddled his hot feet in the wind; he looked down and rubbed his sore shins, and traced the heron's shadow that moved across the ground like a cloud.

Now the limbs were lined up for him. Like steps, they fit his feet, and each one lifted him a little higher. The wind howled and pounced on him and the green limbs around him leaped like surf against the sky. The higher Rudyard got, the harder he held on, with knuckles that were as white as his gritted teeth. If he let go now, there's no telling *where* he might end up, like a sailor swept from his rigging—in Sabathday, perhaps, or Spain, if the wind changed. It was a lot different than climbing in the tower, with no walls here to protect him.

With the wind and the passing clouds, Rudyard felt as if he were turning. It was the strangest feeling; he could hardly keep from letting go—not even knowing if the world turned or he did. He thought it was the world. And there was music in the air! Rudyard couldn't tell from where it was coming, but it wasn't the kind you hear on the radio.

The wind was a streak of blue upon the bay, and as he turned he could see the mailboat churning halfway to Sabathday. Rudyard reversed his field and followed the white wake backward. He barely had time to acknowledge the roofs over Gooseberry Nubble before, through the cemetery woods, his heart rushed home—to where the tower stood on stilts above the barn.

Down in the back meadow, Marmy was sitting on a cushion picking berries, as if she were ripening there in the sun in her red

41

bandanna. Behind her was Parpy's logging road. Now Rudyard had his bearings. Not only was he in Parpy's woodlot, but it came to him, too, that he had never been lost in the first place. In fact, he was standing almost in the top of Parpy's very own landmark tree. He just had never come onto it before from that direction.

How silly he had been, Rudyard thought, looking down at the little patch of woods where fear had filled him with omens and he had run from crows as if they had been wolves. How comical it was; he almost had to laugh; how glad he was that no one else would know!

And now it seemed like being in the tower. Rudyard climbed as if he belonged there, straight up. The mother heron saw him coming and rose to the sky. Her great wings fanned the fiery sun and scattered it through the limbs and across his face. Rudyard stopped like a ground mole caught in the fleet shadow of a hawk when the wings, angry as the sea, washed over him. One swift blow from the bird's beak and he would be a goner. He gritted his teeth with all his might and struck at the bird, holding onto the tree with one hand. He struck at her and struck at her. But still she came, descending on him like an omen. The grim light was burning in her eyes and a banshee in her wings was wailing, "Nest robber! Nest robber!" The bird screamed and dove and drove her beak at him like a hard yellow harpoon, aimed to free his heart from its ribcage.

The next thing Rudyard knew, he stepped off his limb and the whole earth came rushing to his throat. But he had one hand holding on, and, kicking furiously, he got his feet back on a branch. He climbed up between two limbs and wedged himself. If

42

he didn't want to get killed on the first day of summer, then he was going back down. But first he had to do one thing.

Rudyard leaned out over the nest's wide rim and peeked in. He caught his breath. In sticks and soft gray down, the brood was snuggled from the wind. Their wings, bristling with pinfeathers, looked like old feather dusters worn to the naked quills. Rudyard reached out to touch one, but the moment he did the mother teetered on his head. She screamed, *"Gowaaay! Gowaaay!"* And all four of her young ones came alive. They struck at him like snakes, and coiled back their necks and struck at him again. Their beaks clomped shut like wooden clogs, just missing his hand. Their long necks wove from the nest like cobras being charmed from a basket; their beady eyes were glaring in the sun, and they were grunting and grunting.

"My *Lord!*" Marmy would've said. And there they lay . . . exhausted, gawking down their beaks at him like cartoon gooney birds. The mother was raging to the sky.

Rudyard twined his legs around the tree and, as soon as both his hands were free, he reached into the nest. But he pulled back, as if he had poked into a trap. What would Parpy say? But he reached again. And then, as if Marmy had said, *"Ah-ah!* Keep your fingers out of those!"—Rudyard stopped. What would he feed one, anyway? Looking to the clear-blue, mackerel-belly sky, he found his answer! And just in time, too, for the squawking mother had summoned her mate. Rudyard saw him winging in across the bay like a lone gray feather blown by the wind.

One . . . two . . . three, the buttons on Rudyard's shirt popped like tiddly-winks under his tugging. Marmy would think for sure he'd been in a fight. He grimaced, face turned as far away from the clomping beaks as he could get. Even then he closed his eyes. There was no choice of biggest or best. He just snatched the first one that came into his hands. He pulled it to his chest and hugged it and felt it struggle. He held the beak with one hand, and with the other hand he gathered the rest, tucking in the bird's loose ends. He poked the feet in last, as if they were leftovers—while he was sucking in his breath against the warm, bumpy flesh and pin-feathers and the sudden thought of having a hole punched right in the middle of him. But it was too snug in his shirt for the baby heron even to move. He fastened the only button that was left. He started down.

Rudyard scraped himself getting down. But it was a small thing when the sky above him was a storm of wings and terrible squawk-ing, as if he were being attacked by prehistoric lizards. He dangled from the bottom limb and dropped to the ground.

He turned and picked his way expertly through the brush and berry bushes. Buttercups followed him, and Dingbat was leaping at his side. As soon as Rudyard reached the log road, he stopped. He pulled off his shirt and marveled at his plunder. He reached into his pocket for his lucky rock. Clutching it in his fist, he turned and faced back across the clearing. He caught his breath.

"Ain't no ill omens going to catch *us*!" he hollered . . . and ran for all he was worth.

chapter two

The first time Parpy looked up into the tower and saw the bird perched there on the rim, he didn't say a word. He just shook his head. But Marmy, when *she* saw the bird, said it was just such a bird as had perched on Laviticus Beckett's roof, the same day he died. Marmy said that it was a bad omen that killed Laviticus! But Parpy said *nonsense*, dying was the best thing that could have happened to that old cuss.

Anyway, Rudyard had known from the beginning, as far as omens were concerned, that his bird was a good one. There wasn't any doubt. At night Rudyard would go to bed wondering, and in the morning when he woke up, he wondered, too—when the bird flew away, what would happen that was good? But the more he thought, the less he could imagine. Unless his mother and father were coming home.

Slowly, Rudyard's attachment for the bird grew. He spent so much time in the tower that Marmy wanted to know what kind of a spell that bird had over him. And that's what Aunt Lucy wanted to know, too, when she came snooping one Saturday afternoon. When she saw Rudyard climbing to the tower she couldn't wait to tell Marmy that he was idling. And *furthermore*, she predicted, if this was allowed to continue, the town was going to have a young hoodlum on its hands.

Parpy came home from peddling mackerel just in time to be the referee. He said Aunt Lucy only came to stir up a fracas. She ought to go on the radio, Parpy said, so he could turn her off. But Marmy, after she got through listening to Aunt Lucy, as usual didn't know quite what to think. That night Marmy lay awake. And in the morning, as if worried that she really wasn't raising Rudyard right, she put him to work in the garden as soon as he was awake.

Rudyard tried hard to get away by saying, "*Work?* On a *Sunday?*"

But Marmy only waved an arm. "Gardening isn't work," she said.

The sparks flew like flint striking on stones as Rudyard hoed, all the way down the long, long row of corn. His mind was obsessed. At the end of the row, Hey-Diddle-Diddle, the Cat, showed up to greet him. She arched her back like a rainbow and wound herself around his legs. Rudyard bent down to pet her, while she purred as if her engine were idling on full throttle.

The cat was flat now that she had had her kittens. The day Marmy heard them *meaowing* in the loft she had come quick to

48

fetch Rudyard, standing under the tower, clutching her apron full of eggs. While Rudyard climbed down she put the eggs in her pantry, cursing—more kittens. But when she led Rudyard to the barn, and he climbed up and passed them down, she had taken them, one at a time, and pressed them to her heart and blessed them, peeking under their tails—five girls and a boy.

Rudyard glanced at the porch where Marmy was sitting, and he concentrated on the new kittens, as if by thinking hard enough he could suggest to her to go and look at them. But as he thought, a robin bobbed across the garden, searching for worms, and the cat flattened her back and crept off, licking her chops. Rudyard was left leaning on his hoe. He straightened his back, glancing up at the tower.

When Rudyard looked again, Marmy was rocking back and forth, sedately nibbling from the pockets of her apron—cracked corn from one pocket and tea leaves from the other. Rudyard wanted to run. He curled his toes into the warm, rocky soil and looked around for his chance. Dingbat was sprawled in the shade, over on the lawn where the peonies had bloomed, their heavy crimson heads weighed to the ground. He caught Rudyard's eye and winked. But when Rudyard looked back at the porch he knew there wasn't any getting away. Marmy was watching him.

Rudyard stepped back from the row of corn, surveying. What should he do next? The peas invited him, twining about their poles, thin, green pods shining in the sun. Marmy was hoping the pods would fill out so they'd have some peas for the Fourth, but that was only three days away. Rudyard hoped Trim hadn't forgotten to order the watermelon. Parpy always bought one for the

49

Fourth of July. He said watermelon was good, but when *he* was a boy, they celebrated *their* independence with *firecrackers*! He said it was just like the government to make a law against firecrackers. What was a boy supposed to do? But there wasn't any law against banging the screen door, Parpy said, and far as he was concerned, on the Fourth of July, Rudyard could bang it all day if he wanted to.

Rudyard considered the cucumbers, poking his hoe gently among the young vines and parting them. The best thing would be, he was thinking, if he could make the summer last long enough to grow watermelons; although cucumbers were good. Rudyard had already found the first one in the patch that would be ready to pick. It would be a race to see who got to it first—he or Parpy.

There was a patch of squash, and pumpkins, too, and other winter things growing in long rows—potatoes and beets and onions; parsnips Parpy wouldn't dig till spring; and a thin, green raveling of carrots that came undone all the way down the garden.

In the last long row, Marmy had sown sunflowers. She planted them every year, special for the birds that came in flocks to eat the seeds. Marmy said it was good to toll the birds to the garden because while they were there they'd do a job and clean up the bugs. If he hoed the sunflowers first, Rudyard figured, Marmy would be pleased. Maybe then she'd let him go. And so he began.

Parpy had sprinkled wood ashes the length of the row. It drove the flea beetles from the sunflowers, but it didn't phase the slugs. They came in the night, paving their way with crazy little trails of slime, cutting some of the tender shoots clean off and leaving them

50

to wilt in the sun. Parpy noticed this first thing every morning. Marmy said she didn't much mind sacrificing a *few* sunflowers, because she'd planted extras, but Parpy said it broke his heart to see how the slugs destroyed his cucumbers. Marmy said, for sure, everything on earth is put here for a purpose. But Rudyard couldn't think of any purpose there would be for slugs. They *tasted* so bad, for one thing, even the birds turned their beaks up. They weren't like other bugs. Rudyard knew because he had eaten one, once when it didn't get washed from the lettuce. It gagged him the first bite. Marmy said it wasn't polite to spit on the table, but she just said that because she had never bitten into a slug!

After that Rudyard had tasted other bugs. Ants were first. Black ones were a bitter crunch, but he could have made a lunch on the red ones. All of which proved to him that the best things in life taste red, like raspberries and strawberries and watermelon. He had tasted spice bugs, too. He chewed them up in handfuls of warm blueberries, in which they lived. Spice bugs, of course, were bound to taste a little spicy. And so he tried a sourbug—and sure enough, it tasted a little sour. But *nothing* tasted as bad as the slug!

Marmy said it was nasty to eat bugs, but Parpy said it didn't hurt to taste. Marmy said that Parpy said the same thing about his rhubarb wine. Parpy only winked. Tasting bugs was nothing as far as Rudyard was concerned. Everard put a snake's head into his mouth, once—and he dared Rudyard to, as well. But Rudyard said he didn't have to because he had eaten a slug. And if Everard was willing to eat a slug, *too*, then he would be willing to put a

51

snake's head into his mouth. But Everard said he guessed they were even.

Rudyard finished the sunflowers in no time flat. He stiffened his back and stuck out his hoe and looked up again at the tower. The mackerel had been running now since the first day of summer, and Rudyard's gaze fell to the grass where he had stashed some, wrapped in a *Republican Journal.* He wished he were in the tower now, feeding his bird. He wondered what she looked like today. If she grew much bigger, he could harness her to a balloon and they could fly away. He glanced at Marmy, to see if he could go, but still she gave him no sign.

Rudyard leaned on his hoe. He never *used* to have this trouble getting away. At this rate it might take him till noon. He sighed again and put his hoe into the beans. Maybe after he finished *them,* Marmy would let him go. He stooped over and picked a rock off a bean so it could grow straight. One good thing about gypsies, he was thinking—they didn't have gardens. But still he bet they never went without. They probably had watermelons *all* the time, because they were all the time celebrating their independence—which made Rudyard glad he had decided to be one. But just when he was thinking of celebrating his independence, who should come strolling into the yard but Thankful. Everard hadn't been around, it seemed, in a hundred years, but Thankful was around *everywhere.*

Thankful made believe she'd come to visit Marmy, but Rudyard could tell. The first chance she got, she stuck out her tongue and crossed her eyes and stretched her bony neck till Rudyard thought it would snap. He felt like shouting "Rubberneck!" But he knew she was too dumb to insult. She thought she was something, just because she was two years older than he.

"Ain't you going to be late for Sunday School?" Rudyard asked. He hoped Marmy would pick up the hint and send Thankful home. But Thankful was too quick. "Heavens, no," she said. "The bell don't ring yet for another hour."

Rudyard didn't think he could endure for another hour. He fished around in his pocket until he found a root-beer barrel. He brought it out, peeled it, just so, and popped it into his mouth. He twirled it around his tongue and smacked his lips and sucked until his face turned hollow. He knew Thankful wished *she* had a root-beer barrel, too, but instead of drooling, she thumbed her nose and sneered. This was too much for Rudyard. He reached down among the beans and came up with a clod of dirt as big as his fist. All at once he aimed and chucked it.

"*Duck!*" his heart cried. But his lips were frozen. Thankful turned just in time for the clod to *thwack* her, right behind an ear.

"*Ouwwwwwww!*" Thankful howled. It knocked the scowl right off her face. She ran bawling to Marmy. "He . . . he . . . he . . . *hit meeeeee!*"

Rudyard hadn't meant to hit her in the head. *Now* he was going to catch it!

"Land sakes alive," Marmy said. "*Rudyard.* What'd you want to do a thing like that for?"

Marmy only called him by his real name when she was mad. But he was glad she hadn't called him "Plum" in front of Thankful. He stuck up for himself. "She was making rotten faces," he said.

53

"I only hoped her face would *freeze!*"

Thankful whined like a siren.

"The two of you can't get along for a minute," Marmy de-clared. "*Well,*" she steadied herself up out of her chair. "You'll have to settle *this* one amongst yourselves." And she turned and limped away into the house, leaving behind her the screen door slamming like the Fourth of July.

"Why don't you git home?" Rudyard demanded.

"Make me!" Thankful said, and stuck her nose up in spite.

Rudyard stooped for another clod.

"I'm going to tell Mama on you!" Thankful hollered.

"Tell the old President if you want to!" Rudyard took aim.

Thankful grabbed her ear and ran. Rudyard watched her dis-appear down the path with her black hair flying after her. He threw the clod back onto the ground and turned, and Marmy's empty rocking chair was staring him in the eye. His heart leaped like a frog.

Before anybody could catch him, Rudyard was gone.

-2-

Hand over hand Rudyard climbed the ladder, clutching under his chin the newspaper full of fish. Over and over in his mind he repeated the name of his bird, getting it ready on the tip of his tongue. When he reached the top of the tower he popped his head in through the little door and hollered, "Kite!"

The bird greeted him with her appetite, opening her empty gullet toward him as if he were the great blue mother of all

herons. Down in the dark recess of her windpipe, the song was
formed. It came out hoarse and strong, as if someone had thrown
sand into a calliope. Kite advanced toward him and stepped back.
The feathers stood up on her head and the back of her neck. She
advanced again and retreated. She performed for him, like some
old chieftain dressed for a ritual, bowing and strutting. She fluffed
her feathers apart and shook them back.

Rudyard pulled away the newspaper as if unveiling a statue.
The five blue fish shone like the sea. Behind her beak, the bird's
fierce eyes took aim. The sun was just peeping over the rim of the
tower, and in Kite's eyes Rudyard saw his own reflection. Now
that Kite was so tall, Rudyard didn't even have to bend. She
blinked and plucked a fish from his hand. In a graceful gesture she
flipped the fish up over her head and caught it in her beak, stab-
bing out the brain. She swallowed the fish head first. That was so

no fins would scratch, going down. She gulped. The mackerel sank through Kite's gullet like a lead weight.

Kite only ate once a day, but she spent a lot of time regurgitating. She gulped the fifth fish down as if it were her first, coiling her neck like a serpent. When the last fish was gone, Kite was satisfied. She shook herself and began to preen, drawing one shiny feather at a time through her beak.

Rudyard sat down against the wall to watch her. Kite was not a toy he had grown too old to play with. She was real . . . a creature neither of the sky nor of the sea, but both. It was as if she had been caught somewhere in between, and only now was time releasing her to become a bird. It almost seemed that Kite should have gills behind her beak, for she was all ugliness and all beauty at the same time, like some primitive shrine where people come to worship. Rudyard adored the bird. When she flew away it would be as if someone with the power walked up to him to say, "What do you want to be?"

"A gypsy!" he would say.

Just like that. "A gypsy!"

Rudyard stood up and took the long-legged bird in both his hands. He boosted her high over his head. It surprised Kite at first, and she grumbled, deep down in her throat. It was the deepest grumble Rudyard had ever heard.

He put the bird on the rim, propping her legs up under her like stilts. Because Kite was such a collapsible bird, Rudyard waited till she took firm hold, and then he let her go. When he was sure Kite wouldn't fall, he sat back down against the wall to admire her. Kite roosted with her long legs poked up into her chin. Rudyard wondered if he would have to teach Kite about her wings before she would be able to appreciate the sky. If only *he* could be a bird!

Kite rose to her full height. Now she looked complete, standing between the sea and the sky. All she had to do was unfold her wings and the world would be hers. Kite raised one leg as if she were a pink flamingo wading in a swamp in Florida—except she wasn't pink.

Rudyard fished around excitedly in his pocket, feeling through his things until he found his piece of red glass. It had been washed smooth by the tide and he knew it by the touch, so he never once had to take his eyes off Kite. He bent his knee and shined the glass on a patch Marmy had sewn on his dungarees. He slid down onto his back and put the glass to his eye.

The sun traveling across the sky suddenly became red—and Kite, too. She lit up like a candle in front of it. Rudyard had seen a red doe in the orchard—and a red fox. The same doe came every morning during the winter, to muzzle out the apples frozen in the snow. But the fox came only once. Foxes are red, anyway. But a red *deer*! Rudyard was filled with a silent cheer. And now, for the first time anywhere, a *great red heron*!

Kite's throat warbling in the sun reminded Rudyard of Marmy's when she was singing—especially on the high parts. Just then Marmy's voice came calling, "*Heeere*, biddy, biddy, biddy!" And Rudyard thought, at first, that it *was* Kite he heard. But when he realized it wasn't, he jumped up.

He grabbed Kite and started to haul her down. If Marmy saw the bird perched on the rim like that she'd be sure to know where

Rudyard was. But he needn't have worried. When he looked down, Marmy was throwing the orts off the porch. The hens came scrambling for the leftovers. Marmy looked once at the garden where Rudyard wasn't. She shook her head and went back in.

Now that Rudyard had a friend to point out the sights to, there were a few he wanted to be sure to mention. "Over there is where Everard lives," he said, and started the tour. He showed Kite the church and the school and Trim's store, and the wharf where the mailboat was anchored for the day—no mail on Sundays.

"Over there's the cemetery woods," Rudyard continued. "I saw a mange rat coming out of a grave there, once when I was on my way home from school. But he couldn't see me, because he had maggots crawling in his eyes and he was out of his mind bumping into everything. He was a nasty rat."

Rudyard hadn't had anybody to tell his stories to in a long time. He even had one of Parpy's. "And see down there?" He pointed out the farthest roof. "*That's* where Leon Fletcher lives. He don't *ever* take a bath, Parpy says. He don't even swim. And he *hardly* ever changes his socks. Every night before he goes to bed, Parpy says he just throws them up into the air, and if they're stuck up there on his ceiling the next morning, it's time to put on a clean pair."

Rudyard started to tell Kite more, but right in the middle of a breath he stopped.

"Evvv-erard," he heard Aunt Lucy calling.

Rudyard's heart rushed up into his throat as he listened for Everard's answer. Foghorns muffled on the sea called his attention to the fog bank that was rolling in. The sailboats hastened back

toward the harbor's shelter as if the fog would flatten them. He heard the dull roaring surf and the wind pounding, and now and then an outboard motor on some fishing boat—and birds singing, which is what he always listened to when he was up in the tower.

Aunt Lucy called again, "*Evvv*-erard!"

But still there wasn't any answer.

Down across the meadow Rudyard looked where Buttercups was grazing, eating vetch and the heads off daisies, and wild chives that tasted in her milk like onions. But Everard wasn't coming there. Everard wasn't coming by the path, either, nor down along the road where the telephone-light poles stood. Rudyard stared out over the trees. Perhaps Everard would meet him at the crick!

Rudyard snatched Kite down from the rim and set her aside so quickly that she fell over sideways like a toy soldier. He heard her grumbling at him all the way out the door. He took the ladder two rungs at a time. Soon as he could, he jumped to the ground. It sure would be good to see Everard again, he was thinking. And just wait until his cousin heard about Kite!

-3-

Buttercups blatted as she came running, and Dingbat dodged out from under the porch. Down through the meadow they ran—past the animal cemetery and into the alder swamp. Out of the corners of Rudyard's eyes the woods were a blur.

Around a curve they met a woodchuck, and overtook it suddenly. The creature whirled and bared a full, yellow set of teeth into the stampede. Rudyard lost control of his feet as he flew, lightly, through the air. When he came down he buried a toe in the animal's deep, brown fur. It lit a spark that charged his feet and even set his face aglow. And so it wasn't long before he reached the crick.

Rudyard plunged down the bank, driving the seagulls up around him. They went *ky-eying* to the sky like dogs that have been whipped. But Rudyard knew, even before he stepped into the clearing—Everard was nowhere to be seen. He glanced from one green end of the crick to the other. He peered into the water as if his best friend might have drowned. And he had passed up the only perfect chance to catch a woodchuck!

Rudyard stamped his foot and planked himself down in the witch grass. It was no help that Buttercups came, or Dingbat sniffed him—even the dog was unable to console him. Rudyard looked into the water. It would be Aunt Lucy's fault if his socks started rotting to the ceiling. So what if his feet *did* stink? He wasn't going to go swimming alone!

Dingbat whined and pranced back and forth at the edge of the crick, where a yellow scum of clam seed drifted on the tide like pollen carried by the wind. "Stop coaxing," Rudyard complained. "You're all I ever get to go swimming with." But then, because he didn't want to hurt Dingbat's feelings, he got slowly to his feet. It had taken the tide all morning getting in, while the sun had shone hard on the crick's muddy bottom. The water steamed as Dingbat sniffed it.

Rudyard couldn't resist sticking in one toe. Dingbat took it for a sign and plunged in over his head. That made Rudyard forget he didn't want to swim, and in a trance he dropped his suspenders

61

and pulled his T-shirt over his head, unsnapping his pants. His pockets were so full they crashed like cymbals around his feet. It startled him. He stood there naked with the wind browsing over him and Dingbat splashing. The salt spray glistened on his skin and sparkled in his face like bubbles snapping from a glass of ginger ale.

The dog paddle was all Dingbat could do. He circled, looking over his shoulder for Rudyard to follow. The dog paddle was all Rudyard could do, too. That was all Dingbat had taught him. Everard could do the dead-man's float. Rudyard caught himself listening toward the path. He wished Everard could come and teach *him* how to float on his face. More than anything he wanted to tell Everard about Kite. Maybe he could write a note!

Rudyard ransacked his pockets for a pencil. He brought out a jackknife, first; and then a whistle he had whittled from an alder twig; a cunner line was next, with a clam snout still rotting on the hook; there was a key he'd found that he was saving till he could find out what it unlocked; and there was his lucky rock with two milk-white rings of quartz completely around it, like the rings that circle Saturn. The piece of red glass came out almost last; Rudyard dug a little deeper and pulled out the blue marble he had found. It looked as if it might have fallen from the sky. Or it *could* have been a petrified eyeball, in which case it might come in handy when he became a gypsy. But right now it wasn't what he was after.

Rudyard stacked everything on his T-shirt. Then he dug into his other pocket. A horse-chestnut pipe came out first, a piece of chalk he'd saved for writing on rocks came out next, and after that he pulled out a green apple, five kinds of crumbs from Marmy's pantry, and one chocolate chip. Rudyard popped it into his mouth.

Finally he came to his pencil, which was just a stub, way down in the corner. He brought it out and bit it between his teeth. All he needed now was a piece of paper.

Practically at his feet Rudyard found a piece of white bark that had washed up onto the shore. He smoothed the bark over his bare knee, as he bent down. It curled around him as if his leg were a birch tree. He bore down carefully with his pencil as he began.

"Dear Everard."

His printing was good.

"Gess what I have found. It isn't a boat. It isn't a bald eagle, ether. It has a long neck but it isnt a . . ."

Rudyard wrinkled up his nose, "G-u-r . . . g-e-r . . . j-u-r . . . j-e-r?" Rudyard scratched his head. "How do you spell giraffe?" he said out loud, to himself. There wasn't any sense to ask Buttercups. There wasn't even any sense to write a note, anyway, if there wasn't any way for him to deliver it. He threw the pencil down in the grass and waded out a couple of steps and scrootched down until his bottom was wet. And then he set his note afloat and blew it.

The minnows in the crick broke the water like rain while Rudyard bent over his reflection. He flexed one arm, first, and then he flexed the other. He watched his muscles ripple in the sun. When they had first begun to grow, Parpy said a mosquito must have bitten him. And Rudyard almost thought so, too, except they didn't itch.

63

He stood up and looked at the rest of him, wondering—when would he be a man? When he could curse like Parpy would he be a man? Or when he could fight? He looked at his fist, doubled tight—when would it grow? He looked down at his feet. He had Parpy's long legs and knobby knees, Marmy said; and Parpy said he had Marmy's chin, except it wasn't baggy. He had Parpy's chest —*if* he grew some hair on it. He would rather have some whiskers on his chin.

Rudyard bent down closer to look at his face. He had a little bit of a nose that belonged to his mother; he had his mother's eyes, too—according to the picture of her he had seen. He thought probably he had her dreams, although he'd never told anybody about his plans to run away. Rudyard wondered if he looked anything like his father, for he had never seen a picture of him. Aunt Lucy said it was no telling *who* he looked like in that department. She did notice that he had Uncle Harvey's ears. They stuck way out on his head. Aunt Lucy said they were good just for pulling. Rudyard looked at the rest of him. There wasn't much left to be his own.

After awhile Dingbat got tired of swimming alone, and when he saw that Rudyard wasn't going to take the plunge he climbed out and shook himself. He rolled his eyes up and skulked off to lie down in the sun. Pretty soon, Rudyard figured, his bird would be able to go swimming with him. Rudyard had the sudden urge to be back in the tower.

He picked up his pants and climbed into them as fast as he could. He filled his pockets with his things and stretched his suspenders back across his thin brown shoulders. He wound his T-shirt around his neck. He looked at the water once more and he sighed. Swimming alone was too much like taking a bath.

Rudyard dug his toes into the clay and hurried up the bank, but he had only gone halfway when Buttercups butted in front of him. He was prodding her along when he heard someone coming —someone running in shoes, so he knew it wasn't Everard. Rudyard knuckled a hole on Buttercups' neck and dragged the goat with him, off into the thick brush where he crouched. There in the dark shade around him some lady's-slippers bloomed, soft veined sacks of pink that were hung on slender stems—such a peculiar flower and so rare that Marmy had warned him about the law against picking them. But Rudyard didn't even notice them until Buttercups ate one, which distracted him only for a second. He took hold of the goat by her chin. Buttercups stopped her chewing and tuned her ears to the footsteps that were pounding closer on the path. They both peeked out, anxiously wondering who it was that came this way—and Thankful appeared.

Thankful was gripping at her side a clod of earth that was ten times bigger than her fist. She braced herself and slid a little down the slippery bank, passing so close to Rudyard that he had all he could do to keep from jumping out and terrifying her. But he could tell by the way she walked that she was looking to get even. Rudyard held his breath.

Rudyard waited for just the right moment before he stepped out. When he did Thankful was far below him, at the bottom of the bank. He cupped his hands into a megaphone to aim his voice. He took her by surprise.

"*Rubberneck!*" he hollered.

66

And just in time. The church bell started:

Donggg!

Donggg!

Donggg! . . . reverberating in the Sunday air like the echo of the grave calling out to all the sinners.

Rudyard bolted with his goat. He never even glanced back. He just shifted his feet into high gear and took off. All he wanted was to see his bird, and be back safe in the tower.

chapter three

One by one the days crept past. It seemed that each of them was a little longer than the one before—but Everard never came by. Rudyard watched for him from the tower, but all he saw was Uncle Harvey's lobster boat putting out in the morning, and then at night he saw it putting in. Often he thought of going down there, and twice he went—but the vision of Aunt Lucy stopped him. Both times Rudyard fled back past the graveyard, escaping through the woods while there was still light. Both times the tower was a welcome sight.

Kite grew so fast that Rudyard had to add more fish to her diet—one, at first; and eventually, three more to satisfy her appetite. Every time he measured her, Rudyard wondered—when would she be as big as he was? The day when Kite came feather-perfect to his chin, she spread her wings and hopped up onto the rim of the tower. There she stood, overlooking her domain—and never once, after that, did she offer to come down. When Rudyard brought the fish, he had to pass them up, and she'd bend down and spear them.

Thankful came one day like a little sharp-nosed shrew, her neck stretched and her eyes bulging up from the meadow. Rudyard figured for sure that *she* would tell Everard about Kite. He stayed up in the tower all that night waiting for Everard to come, listening to the bass frog throbbing from the spring. Out over the bay he watched the lights straggling in from Sabathday. He watched the dawn come over the sea. It chased the stars away. He watched Uncle Harvey and Everard putting out for another day of lobstering. And a gray day it was, too, until the sun burned through. He turned to his bird.

"It doesn't really matter so much, now that I got you, whether I got a best friend or not," he said. "You will do."

By the end of July summer had started to fade, or so Rudyard figured, as he stood in the tower and watched it. The meadow had been mowed, and in the place of green, the dry brown windrows could be seen. Looking at it from the tower, the only bright patch that showed up was the animal cemetery, down where the spring overflowed into the alder swamp. The monarch butterflies still flitted over the milkweed there; the fireweed was flaring in the sun; and the yellow St. John's wort was in bloom.

In the garden, Marmy's giant sunflowers opened, another sign of just how old summer was getting. The watermelon seeds were up, where Rudyard had spit them off the end of the porch, though they wouldn't have time to amount to much. They reminded Rudyard of the cucumber patch, and when he went to look—sure enough! The first cucumber was waiting to be picked. He snapped it off the vine and hurried away to the tower to eat it and be entertained by the view.

As Rudyard munched the juicy cucumber he looked down to where the barn door was pushed open on its rollers. Inside the dark barn he could see Parpy, hunched over in a chair, shucking quahogs. The locust blossoms trailed in the wind like lace, past the place where Parpy's legs stuck out. His jackknife was glinting. Hey-Diddle-Diddle, the Cat, had lugged her kittens down from the loft, all of them fat on young robins and full of milk. They pawed among the shells Parpy was dropping between his feet. They gnawed on the sweet meats and snouts they caught like flies as Parpy slatted them from his blade.

Parpy had said yesterday that what ailed Aunt Lucy was, she needed to go off and get some women's liberation. Marmy smirked and said she didn't know, but now that he had mentioned it, maybe that was what ailed *her*, too. Parpy said he hoped not at her age! Marmy said you're only as old as you feel. So Parpy was fixing supper today, and Marmy had taken her handle dipper and a ten-quart pail and gone off into the woods to pick some berries. As far as Rudyard could tell, they were going to have one of Parpy's specials—quahog stew, and new corn picked from the garden while it was still only sweet blisters, with some of Marmy's thick slices of buttered bread, no doubt. And, if Marmy came home in time, they'd have fresh raspberries, too.

After he was through shucking the clams, Parpy would pound

71

up the shells to feed to the hens so they could turn them into calcium to produce thick shells for their eggs. Rudyard was glad he could get all the calcium *he* needed from goat's milk, though he guessed it was easier for hens to eat crushed shells than it would be for him—because hens don't have any teeth, Marmy said. And Rudyard had looked. Marmy showed him when she was cleaning one that all a hen has is a gizzard, which is filled with sand.

The cucumber juice trickled down Rudyard's chin. He knew a lot about hens. Parpy said you can always tell about a hen, how full her egg-bag is, by the way she sings. The only thing Rudyard *didn't* like about hens was walking barefoot where they had been —and they had been everywhere. Parpy never would lock them up. He said he'd rather see them running free. He never worried about them scratching up the garden because he had Dingbat trained to keep an eye out. *But,* Parpy said, even if he didn't have Dingbat for control, he'd still let the hens run loose—the way the Japanese did. It makes more sense to fence in the garden than the birds, Parpy said, even when the birds are only hens. As long as the hens run free, they get more to eat and their yolks stand up brighter. Parpy said *he* was an *organic* farmer.

Rudyard chomped the cucumber to its bitter end. He ate that, too, and left only the stem, which he dropped. He watched it disappear through the air before it hit the ground. The hens came scrambling and squabbled over it as if they'd uncovered a worm. Rudyard wondered what Parpy would say when he discovered the cucumber was gone. A cucumber wasn't much, except when it was the first one. Rudyard burped. Maybe he could blame it on the hens.

Rudyard sat down with his back against the wall. He wiped his chin and rolled his eyes up toward Kite. On days like this, when he missed Everard the most, he could hardly wait for his bird to fly away. Then he would become a gypsy. When that happened, the first place he wanted to go was Florida. If there were gypsies anywhere, it would be in Florida—because gypsies like it where it's hot. And if Kite was looking for a hot place, she might migrate to Florida, too. "Parpy says in Florida you can swim even in the winter," he told his bird.

Of course, he wouldn't stay in Florida for long. No gypsy would —not with the world so *full* of places to go. Kite hunched and grumbled and tucked her wings, while Rudyard studied her as if she were a travel portfolio. He wanted to see the street canals of Venice, for one thing, and ride in a gondola to where there are statues running with wings on their feet. For another, he wanted to see the men in India who walk barefoot on beds of burning coals. He squnched up his toes just thinking about it. He wanted to see a Fiji Islander, too—Marmy said sometimes he looked like one. He wanted to see the Loch Ness monster and the Red Sea, and he wanted to go to China and ride in a rickshaw—like Parpy used to ride him in the wheelbarrow over bumps before he grew too heavy. There is a tribe in Africa, Parpy had said, that lived on goat's milk and cattle blood. Rudyard wanted to see them, too, even though he knew he wouldn't care too much for cattle blood. Parpy didn't suppose *he* would be too fond of it, either. Rudyard liked about the same things Parpy liked—except tripe. While he was in Africa, Rudyard figured, he might meet a witch doctor, too, for that was another thing—he wanted to see some magic. Parpy had seen a woman sawed in two, on stage, in front of five hundred paying people, once. And it hadn't phased the woman a bit. Rudyard closed his eyes and dreamed. He wanted to go where boomerangs came back to people and bagpipes played. In Bucksport, Parpy said, there was a gravestone with a witch's foot growing right out of it, and every time they cut the foot off it grew right back. That's the kind of stuff Rudyard wanted to see, with maybe a carnival with belly dancers and duckbilled platypuses and a Siamese twin or two.

Somewhere in between, Rudyard figured, he was bound to run into his mother and father. Just thinking about it got him so excited he couldn't see. But then he remembered that his eyes were shut. He opened them up. He was almost in a rapture as he looked at his bird. "Oh, *please!*" he said. "When will it happen?"

And no sooner had he said it than . . .

BOOM!

Something happened.

It rattled the brain in Rudyard's head, and his eyes flew to the sky like little startled birds. As he jumped up, he heard Parpy charge out of the barn, raving at the government. Parpy looked at the government the same way Marmy looked at the devil, as if it were something that would get him. Parpy blamed *everything* on the government, including the fact that there wasn't a kettleful of flounders left in the whole bay. "Not a kettleful!" Parpy would say. "You can't blame it on the fishhawks!" And now he shook his fist at the sky, the way he had once when Marmy warned him he was tempting providence. Aunt Lucy knew words like aggravating and excruciating and intolerable, but Parpy's words were sharp and quick.

Buttercups ran off into the woods, bleating and flicking her ears, while Dingbat hauled himself out from under the porch and began to wail. The rooster stepped among his hens. It could have been the end of the world. Rudyard cringed as if a bomb had been dropped. He squinted at the sky. He opened his mouth and clasped his hands. He hadn't been this happy since he learned to fly! He opened up his mind and soared, up where a thin, silver sliver tracked across the sky, trailing a banner through the blue as if of chewed-up clouds. The jet had broken the sound barrier.

Kite straddled the tower rim and craned her neck against the sky. *"Grawwk! Grawwk!"* she screamed at that which could fly higher and make more noise than she.

-2-

The jet streak was barely melting in the sky when Marmy came trudging up across the meadow. She rode her hips up the path from the woodlot as though they were a horse. When she got halfway, she stopped and set the pail down and stood so her big shadow protected the berries from the sun. She waved up at the tower, *yoo-hooing* like the wind.

Rudyard ducked out the door and scuttled down. By the time he reached Marmy, Buttercups was there. "Now you git!" Marmy was saying. She thumped her foot and threatened to bonk the goat with her dipper. "I've told you before," she said, "I don't appreciate goats!" She stood her ground, a small bouquet of strawflowers she had gathered thrusting from her bosom. Marmy had treasures buried in her bosom that the pirates had never heard of, Parpy said. Parpy said when God made Marmy, He used an extra pat of mud in her heart—and an extra pat in her foot. Marmy thumped her foot again for good measure.

Above her sunburned cheeks, Marmy adjusted her bandanna. Her face was flushed to the bone. "That awful sound," she said. "Last time we had one of those it broke up the hen and we lost the whole setting of eggs, and the time before that it dried up the goat. This time it knocked the berries off the vines and drove the yellow jackets out of their nests in a swarm, and the next thing I hear is that grandfather of yours with his tongue raining curses down onto the neighborhood for God and everyone else to hear!"

Rudyard could see that Parpy needed defending. "He was only spouting-off," Rudyard said.

"*Spouting-off!*" Marmy was exasperated. "What would Aunt Lucy say?"

Rudyard shrugged. Marmy needn't tell *him* about what Aunt Lucy said.

Marmy seemed off guard, but the instant Buttercups took one step toward her pail—"*Git!*" she said, and tapped the goat so that she almost popped the enamel on her dipper. "Now I've warned you once. I've warned you twice—keep your nose clear of these berries or you'll lose it."

Marmy looked a trifle spent. "I've been out in the sun too long. Don't let on to your grandfather," she confided, "but I ain't as kipper as I used to be. If you want something special made with these berries. Plum, you'll have to hurry now and lug me some water." Marmy was fussing. "My feet feel as if they're on their way home from the fireman's ball." Marmy looked down. "It's a mystery to me," she declared, "why anybody who likes to dance

76

would be cursed so with corns."

"Here," Rudyard said, and took the bucket. "Let me help." He waited while Marmy slipped off her shoes before he led the way, up across the meadow. Marmy followed with her shoes dangling in one hand and the dipper in the other. Marmy's feet were blue. Rudyard looked down self-consciously at his own two feet. They were black. Probably tonight Marmy would make him wash them.

The pail was just heavy enough to make him feel strong, and so he swaggered as he walked, his muscles bulging. He took the liberty of tasting one of the berries—but only one. Buttercups kept butting in front of him, till Marmy cleared the way. "Everytime I look at you, you're eating," she said to the goat. Rudyard looked at her to see if she meant him.

Up where the locust blossoms were dripping on the lawn, Rudyard stopped. He had to rest. He cleared his throat and put the bucket down, then propped one hand up on his hip. He used his other hand as a shield against the sun. He squinted through the limbs to the rim of the tower, absorbed in the great blue heron. His bird stood slate gray against the great blue sky.

Marmy stopped and propped an elbow up onto her hip and looked, too. "It's a funny thing," she said. "But from where I was picking today, I would've sworn that crane's nest was empty. Them birds must've all struck out on their own."

"What do you suppose is keeping Kite?" Rudyard asked, though he could about guess. She would leave when it was time.

Marmy lowered an eye. "What do *you* suppose?" she said.

"Well . . ." Rudyard thought. "She ain't learned to fly."

Marmy frowned. "You think that's it?"

77

Rudyard shrugged. "Maybe it's the food," he said—when all the time he knew what Marmy was alluding to. Marmy was still trying to tell him that Kite might be a bad omen. He wanted to tell Marmy the truth about what was on his mind, but he couldn't just up and say, "Look! I think I'm going to become a gypsy, which means I'll be going away to stay where I can hang around with other gypsies." When he came right down to it, there wasn't any sense for him to stay on the island any longer. He couldn't even hang around with *Everard*, here. And he had this awful urge, lately, to be off somewhere gallivanting.

Marmy gave her foot that extra pat when she mounted the porch. That was to inform Parpy that she was home. It jarred the windows in the house and sent the chickens out into the sun, scurrying in puffs of dust. Marmy held the screen door open just enough to get through, barring the way for all goats. She made a grand gesture as Rudyard entered. He set the pail down in her kitchen, while Marmy went to the cupboard where she kept her money cup.

As soon as her back was turned, Rudyard seized his chance. One ripe, red berry had only tantalized his appetite. The next time Marmy looked, secretly, inside his mouth, his tongue was crushing out the juice from a whole handful. It took every bit of his will power to keep from smacking.

Marmy extended a nickel. "Here's for a good helper," she said. Rudyard bowed his head and took the money gratefully.

Marmy looked down busily at his feet. "Better lug enough water for washing *two* pair of feet," she said. "Unless you want yours spit shined." She took him by the hair and turned his head

gently to inspect his ears, clucked, and let him go. "Hustle your-
self along, Plum," she said. "See that you don't dilly-dally at
Trim's store. By the time you're home, Parpy'll have supper on.
He's depending on you this evening, you know, to help him haul
the net. He says the big ones put up more of a fight than what they
used to."

Rudyard was prancing to be gone. The wild sweet in his mouth
was driving him.

"And don't fill up on culch, either," Marmy said, "which
means," she finished all in a rush, "keep-the-peanut-butter-cups-
out-of-you-or-you'll-spoil-your-appetite!"

"*Um*," Rudyard said on his way out the door, savoring his berries.

Rudyard stopped by the barn to pick up a pail, and down
through the meadow he ran, playing with his nickel. Buttercups
bounced beside him, and Dingbat was catching up. Rudyard was
thinking: When he got to the store, he would tap his money on
the glass candy counter for Trim to come and wait on him. He
would order one Tootsie Roll, one piece of bubblegum, one twist
of licorice (*red*), one root-beer barrel, and two chocolate kisses
wrapped in silver foil. But with so many good things to choose
from, it was hard, once he started looking, not to change his mind.
In place of the root-beer barrel, for instance, he might just rather
have a slice of sugared bacon, even though it wouldn't last so
long.

Rudyard watched the pail's shadow blipping over the windrows
as he walked. The meadow was all stubble under his feet; where

79

the earth was scalped the sun shone hot and sweet, drying out the herbs which had been raked to ripen with the hay—goldenrod and yarrow and Queen Anne's lace. With the air balmy off the sea, Rudyard forgot all about supper. If he hurried he could be at the wharf in time to see the passengers stepping off the mailboat. Summer people were always a sight. And with so many coming and going, who was to say there wasn't a gypsy among them? You never can tell where one of *them* will show up!

Dingbat's long ears were slapping time with Buttercups' bag, and there was the labor of the dog's breathing. But still there was another sound. An avalanche of wings closed over Rudyard's head. He expected to see an eagle when he looked up, though Parpy said the government had put all of *them* on dollar bills. Instead of an eagle, a great blue heron stepped out of the sky and stood beside him.

Rudyard jumped. *"Kite!"*

"Grawwk!" said the bird.

Rudyard spun around to the tower, looking at the rim, as if he couldn't believe that it was empty. *"Yippeeeee!"*

Rudyard threw his pail up into the air. It hit the ground, clanging in the wind. Buttercups and Dingbat came back to see what was the matter. Parpy said they'd make a motley crew—a dog and goat and a great blue heron, and a boy whose yellow hair streamed when he ran. Kite chased him now, down between the windrows, flapping her wings—and Rudyard was flapping his arms.

Kite's shadow blurred along over the hay as if she were taking off down a runway for jets. Suddenly, she left the ground with

nothing in her wings but air. Rudyard forgot he wasn't a bird. He was so filled with the desire that *he* almost flew away, too!

"Flap!" he hollered. *"Flaaap!"*

Kite toddled on new wings, as though, if she tipped one way or the other, she would spill. She leveled off and flew—straight out over the meadow.

Rudyard threw out his arms to embrace the wind. He hollered, "BOOM!"

chapter four

Every day after Kite learned to fly, Rudyard expected she would be gone. But every morning when he looked, the bird was fixed to the tower like a weathervane, her beak still pointing to the wind. The only time Kite went anywhere was when she followed Rudyard, fishing and swimming and on expeditions. She followed him everywhere. Down across the meadow her wide wings shuffled above his head. Through the alder swamp she strode beside him, interested in everything he was interested in. They explored the rim of the shore together at low tide, and when the tide was high they played wave-tag. In the morning, Kite went with him to lug the water for Marmy to soak her corns, and in the afternoon Kite followed him with Parpy when they went to haul the net. Parpy liked the bird. He didn't even mind when she hopped down off the boat's stern and devoured his mackerel—sixty-cents-worth at a time.

83

Kite grew till Rudyard could look her square in the eye. He thought it was good to have a friend, and when she flew he only wished that he could fly, too. But he couldn't figure it out: Why didn't Kite fly away? The hummingbirds had left *their* nests, though they came regularly with their wings whirring to suck the nectar from Marmy's evening primrose; the swallows in the barn were on *their* own, perching in a long row the length of Marmy's clothesline; and the crows had left *their* nests. Rudyard could hear them in the woods with their gullets open, gargling the wind. Even the polliwogs in the spring had grown legs and dropped their tails and hopped off into the swamp to sing. And August was half gone!

One day when Rudyard thought he couldn't wait any longer for Kite to fly away, he decided to make the tower into a ship. And so he rigged a sail in it. He used Marmy's clothespole for a mast—and for a sail, Marmy's sheet, which he stole just to try. But up came the wind and broke the whole thing and swept away Marmy's sheet in a gale, and Marmy's pole, too, out over Gooseberry Nubble, and out to sea. And Rudyard imagined he was shipwrecked.

It was on a morning when the wind was right that Rudyard woke to the crying of the shore birds. He crawled out from under his warm quilt and climbed into his pants, shaking off the morning chill. He spent a long time in Marmy's pantry, picking out eight silver fish from the sinkful. He also had in mind something sweet and plentiful, but Marmy sensed what he was up to. When Rudyard turned, she filled the doorway, standing with her arms akimbo. *"Tut-tut,"* Marmy said.

84

Rudyard stood on the porch and waited, curling his toes in the warm sun. He expected his bird to fly right down. When she didn't, he looked up, searching the tower's rim. The handle of the bucket slipped from his hand. The rim was empty.

Rudyard's heart almost flew him up the ladder. He drew himself onto the platform in a hurry, bucking his shins as he crawled through the little door. It felt strange to enter the tower without receiving a greeting. He scrambled up and hung his chin out over the rim and looked to the ground. He looked up and around. But Kite was nowhere to be seen.

Rudyard stood back and braced himself, waiting for the moment of magic to descend. Now his fortune should be told. Would it shake him? He let go of the tower's rim and sat down. He crossed his legs and crossed his arms. Would it start and overtake him all of a sudden, or would it creep up gradually from behind? He bowed his head and made himself ready to be transformed. With what would it fill him? Rudyard waited. He closed his eyes and sat in the dark. And waited. But not a twinge.

Perhaps Marmy was right, a little voice said. Rudyard peeked out at his skin. *"Well?"* he wanted to say—he wasn't dead, yet.

Rudyard looked up at the sky. The sky was the same. At least, it still covered his head. He looked back down, dumbfounded. The same sky; the same skin; he looked around him at the same tower. Only one thing was changed. Then came the sad realization that he was alone. He had owned a bird, once, but she was gone. He had only wanted Kite gone if it was going to change him, but since he was the same, he wanted her back. His belief in magic was ruined. He stood up, dazed.

86

Out over the plain of the sea, Rudyard looked, where the waves merged with the bright blue sky. Uncle Harvey's lobster boat created a din in his ears. Everard blurred through his tears, just putting out for another day of lobstering. Rudyard shook his head as if waking from a dream. It didn't seem possible that Kite would fly away to Florida and leave him. He backed out through the little door as quickly as he could. While the tears were still drying on his feet, Rudyard hurried down the ladder and went searching.

Dingbat followed him, and Buttercups tagged along in their tracks—though she was hardly concerned. She was reluctant in the first place, but she came, looking back at the orchard where the ripe yellow apples lay bruised on the ground. When they reached the crick, down under the bank where the jewelweed grew ten feet tall, Rudyard sat himself upon a rock to wait for the tide to go out.

They weren't there long before Rudyard took out his red glass. He squinted through it at the sky, but that pacified him only for a minute. He rummaged through his pocket and came out with his alder whistle. He tooted it. He dug down into the corner for his petrified eyeball—he'd known all the time that it was only another blue marble. He ran it around his mouth a few times, and took it out, wet and shining. He threw the marble, as high and as far as it would go. It plopped into the water like a piece of blue sky. He took his chalk out, next, and wrote on a big rock: K-I-T-E. It looked like a monument to a great blue heron.

After that he threw some rocks, selecting each one absently. He threw a red one full of iron ore that went *ka-plunk* when it hit the water; he chose a gray piece of slate that skipped eleven times; he launched a gigantic piece of white quartz, and a piece of granite with mica flecks that sparkled in the sun like fool's gold; and a piece of limestone, next. His teacher knew everything there was to know about rocks, but he had *never* seen her throw one.

The farther the tide went out, the harder Rudyard threw—till after awhile his arm grew lame. All that remained was the shallow pool where he had seen Kite's mother feeding. Rudyard balanced on the cool, wet rocks as he walked down the shore. He waded into the pool and stood there, ankle deep. He wondered what to do next. Shielding his eyes, he looked up at the sky—hoping to see Kite's sharp wings come scissoring over the jagged tree line. But all he saw were crows and one small sea duck flying in a straight line. The minnows came to nibble his feet and twitch like nerves when he wiggled his toes. He bent over some periwinkles that were grazing like sheep in the deep green algae on a rock. The rock rose up out of the water like a hillside. At the bottom of the hill a drift of white barnacles spread out, casting their nets into the water like tiny fishermen. He even saw one barnacle which had welded itself securely to the back of a shining black periwinkle—and there it lived, and rode, moving at a powerful snail's pace. Rudyard marked it down in his head as the only barnacle he had ever seen that traveled. Probably it had been around the rock a hundred times, Rudyard figured. He wondered if the barnacle thought that it had seen the world. And that made him think of gypsies, which reminded him of Kite, which started him to thinking all over again.

89

This was the only place in all the world where Rudyard might expect to find a great blue heron. He was reluctant to leave it. He turned, looking to the trees—up where the green limbs silently brushed the sky. He shielded his eyes. Except for the sun, the sky was empty, and Kite was nowhere to be seen.

On his way home Rudyard lingered in the woods just long enough to kick a stump. It fell apart, and the sowbugs came tumbling out of the rotting wood like tiny, brittle armadillos. Rudyard fell down on his knees to gather them, poking them all to hump them up. He drew a circle in the deep shade beneath the hackmatacks. He put his sowbugs into it, as if they were marbles. The game started out with six, and it was like juggling, keeping them all going at once—but Rudyard's mind wasn't really on it. One by one, before he knew what was happening, his marbles had all quit and walked away. He stood up and scuffed out the circle with his bare feet.

As he walked, Rudyard looked up through the trees, as if there might be something there he hoped to see. But there wasn't. He passed a brown snake stretched out in the sun warming its blood, its pink tongue lashing from its head. Ordinarily he would have stopped to dangle the snake by its tail, but not today. Dingbat pointed the way—at a mouse and a toad and seven butterflies, more or less, flitting through the woods. But Rudyard paid no attention. Buttercups deserted him because he was no fun. She went off into the woods, sticking her head out of the brush every once in awhile to see if he had changed.

Rudyard's search brought him again to the animal cemetery, where long, limber stalks of joe-pye weed and cattails stood. He sank down into the grass and drew up his knees.

A daddy-longlegs boarded Rudyard from a bay leaf and scrab-
bled up his pantleg. Rudyard lowered his arm automatically, like
a drawbridge, and lifted the little creature up. It looked like a
Martian, with its round, brown body dangled in the center of
eight nimble legs. But the legs reminded him of Kite, and he
brushed the daddy-longlegs aside and got up with a lump in his
throat as big as his fist.

Rudyard looked all day. He stopped to stir up the eel in the
spring. The frog was gone. Later on he even peeked into the rain
barrel to see how the mosquitoes were doing. He saw a few hooked
larvae squiggling in the reflection of his sorry face.

It was late in the afternoon when Rudyard climbed back into
the tower. The flowers were closing in the shadow of the mountains. Red and purple was the sunset, branded on his face with
worry. He might as well make up his mind, Rudyard figured—he
probably never would see Kite again, any more than he would
ever see his mother and father. He hung his head. Kite had been
his only reason to stay because he had wanted to find out if she was
good or bad or *what* she meant. But now he knew she didn't mean
anything at all. She was gone and he could run away. There wasn't
anything more to keep him.

Rudyard watched Uncle Harvey's lobster boat putting in, and
the next thing he knew it was getting dark. The evening star came
out, flickering like a candle at the edge of night; the lights began
to come on out over Gooseberry Nubble. It was very quiet, now—
much more so than it had been before. Only the wind's ominous
voice was everywhere, while the waves were crowding on the

91

shore. And old Miss Jake was swooning her cats home to eat. Her sweet heart was trembling in her throat.

Rudyard climbed down slowly from the tower. He stood for awhile on the porch, in the light from the window. Still in the pail, heads first, were the eight silver fish with their oily tails drooping out like mustaches. He could hear Marmy moving about in her kitchen. Supper was over. Parpy had gone fishing alone and come back. Rudyard hesitated to go in. He hadn't even lugged Marmy's corn water.

"A-men," Marmy said when she saw him. "It's about time." But she took one look at his face. "Dear soul," Marmy crooned, sorry she had said a thing.

Parpy beckoned him, "Pull up a chair, Plum."

And Marmy offered to bring him a glass of goat's milk. "And a piece of chocolate cake," she said.

But Rudyard only shook his head. He stood before the china closet, looking in at Marmy's jug with the great blue heron sweeping across it that came all the way from China. After awhile he turned and silently climbed upstairs to the dark garret.

-2-

Rudyard didn't bother to undress. He might never undress in this house again, he thought, as he listened to Marmy tidying up her kitchen. Would she miss him? She had told him once, no matter *what* Aunt Lucy said, *she* thought he was the salt of the earth. Marmy had been the only real mother he had known. She let him dunk his apples in the honey, didn't she? He never even had to ask—not like Everard's mother made *him* do. Rudyard could even dunk a cucumber in the honey, if he wanted to. And he could drink tea. Marmy even poured it for him. Aunt Lucy said if she caught *Everard* drinking tea, then *he* would get the licking of his life—Rudyard couldn't figure out why. Aunt Lucy, herself, drank tea. He wondered what she'd say if only she knew that he had tasted wine. Or what would Marmy do? But that was his and Parpy's secret. He was sorry he wouldn't be around to mend Parpy's water tower, but he guessed they would make out okay lugging their water from the spring. Rudyard tossed onto his back and listened to the bedsprings creaking.

Run away, the bedsprings seemed to say—*run away, run awaay, run awaay*!

All Rudyard could see in the dark were the shadows of the sweet herbs Marmy had hung in bunches under the eves to dry—catnip for the cat to perk her up in the middle of winter, and sage for stuffing chickens, and horehound to brew with honey to make what Marmy called her cough syrup concoction. In the warm summer air the herbs were withering—in the drowsy, scented night as Rudyard lay there. He wished he'd never taught the bird to fly.

He wished until he closed his eyes and breathed deep and started drifting off. But through the night a mosquito came, vaguely whining, like a siren he had heard from the mainland once when the wind was right. And just as the mosquito settled down quietly to drill his blood, a rock came knocking on the roof. It startled Rudyard. He hurried to the window and leaned out.

"*Hey!*" The voice whispered in the night, above the wind sizzling in the locust leaves.

"Who is it?" Rudyard inquired.

"Me."

"Me who?"

"*Mee!*" the voice insisted.

"Everard?"

"Come on down."

Rudyard almost fell out through the window, he went so fast. He crawled across the shed roof and leaped to the ground. "*Everard!*" he said, and hugged him till his best friend grunted. "What're *you* doing here?" he said. "And where've you *been* all summer? Why didn't you come sooner?"

"Mama said if she knew of it, she'd blister my hide," Everard said—not mentioning the graveyard, which, of course he must have run through, judging by the way he was panting. "I couldn't stay away nomore," he said.

Rudyard stepped back to look. Everard was gaunt as a fox, with his sharp, fox nose sticking out in the night. He had a cowlick, too, that stood up like fox ears on the top of his head.

"I come to say good-bye," Everard said, and looked around him as if he were being hunted.

"How did *you* know I was leaving?" Rudyard said.

Everard set him straight. "I didn't come to say good-bye to *you*; I come to say good-bye to *me*!"

"Where you going?"

"I don't know." Everard swallowed hard.

"What's the matter?" Rudyard asked.

"Someone's plundering Papa's lobster traps and he's taking it out on me. He's awful mean to be working with," Everard said. "And when I get home at night, Mama don't help much."

"Then run away with me!" Rudyard was suddenly excited.

"Where *you* going?"

"Florida," Rudyard said—"for a start."

"*Florida!*" Everard echoed. "What's there?"

Rudyard looked around. "Come on," he said. "Let's go where we can talk."

They went out onto the road, into the night that was lit only by the distant moon on the edge of the sea. But soon even the moon was lost behind the trees as they moved downhill. Then there were only the lightning bugs, and the stars in the sky that showed brighter than chickweed blossoms clustered against the black earth. The stones made coarse walking for their calloused feet, for Everard was barefoot, too. Dingbat stayed behind, sprawled out under Marmy's kitchen stove, but Buttercups made herself welcome, walking on her toes and softly sniggering, like a deer—or a unicorn, if unicorns snigger. As they walked, Rudyard talked about his summer and how he had found a bird he thought was an omen—and the only reason he had stayed around *this* long was to find out what she meant.

"But you can't be a gypsy," Everard said, when Rudyard came to that part.

"I *can't!*" Rudyard said, as if he didn't believe it. "How come?"

"Such things don't even exist nomore," Everard said, as if surprised that Rudyard didn't know.

"Not around *this* part, they don't," Rudyard said. "But how about Away?"

95

"They don't exist there, neither," Everard said.

"Who said they don't?"

"Mama said."

"You mean," Rudyard asked, "there ain't no more sea captains and their ain't no more gypsies, *either*?"

Everard shook his head. "That's what Mama said. Besides," he added, "I don't want to go to Florida, anyway."

"How come?"

"Because it's too far."

"It ain't too far," Rudyard contradicted.

"Oh-yes-it-is, if we didn't bring our shoes," Everard said. "And we didn't."

"Then what *could* we do?" Rudyard challenged.

Everard didn't even have to think. "We could join the army," he said.

Rudyard groaned. "I don't want to belong to no army," he said.

"I do," said Everard.

"Well, I don't," said Rudyard.

"What *would* you belong to then?"

"I might belong to the *Salvation* Army," Rudyard said. "Marmy said that's the only decent army to belong to, nowadays."

Both boys grew quiet as they came to the cemetery woods. The road cut through in a wide swarth as if the grim reaper had just passed there before them. They looked out the corners of their eyes and stepped along, both waiting for the other to change his mind. But they were together, and pretty soon they came to the church. It stood out over them like a black thing with its shoulders hunched. They ran as far as the school. *"Phew!"* Rudyard said, when they stopped. "That was hot-footing it!"

Beyond the school, bright windows lit the way, and lights fell out in squares on little garden patches and framed them in soft tapestries of marigolds and pinks and small white single poppies. They weren't afraid—until they came to Everard's house. They sneaked by with their breath held tight in their throats, as if Aunt Lucy were hiding with a butcher knife behind the lilac bush.

Trim's store came next. It was open late. Buttercups went up to the window and reared back on her hind legs and put her front legs against the sill as she stared in at all that was happening. The boys looked in, too, and saw the men sitting around on nailkegs, spinning their yarns. Buttercups stuck her lip against the glass and snorted, and the two boys scattered across the road. They ran to the wharf and squatted up under it, crawling on their hands and knees over the boulders. It was a safe place, and soon as Rudyard was situated in a comfortable position he bent his knees up under his chin and began to pick his toes. He began wondering, too, about what Everard had said about gypsies. If it was as true about gypsies as it was about sea captains, then the world must be getting to be a different place.

"I guess I won't run away after all," Rudyard said.

Everard was disappointed. "How come?"

The mailboat chaffed against her lines and the tide sloshed around the pilings under the wharf. "I just changed my mind," Rudyard said.

"Well, I ain't changed mine."

"You going alone?"

"I don't see nobody else to go *with* me."

"And you don't mind?"

Everard didn't answer.

The moon came up like a big red balloon filled with hot air. In its light the seals grew brave and crawled up out of the sea. Their wet fins slapped on the rocks as they moved in close around the two boys. Rudyard almost felt as if the seals had heard them talking, so softly the creatures began to grunt. Rudyard wondered what advice they were offering. As he listened, a loon's voice cracked the night, laughing pitifully, as if it, too, had caught wind of something that was being said, as if it knew exactly what Rudyard was feeling, and Everard, too.

Rudyard dug down deep into his pocket. "Here," he said, and offered Everard a going-away present.

His cousin took it. "What is it?"

"Hold it up and see."

Everard put the red glass to his eye. The moon floated in the sky like a big, red bubble blown from a burning wand. "*Wow!*" he said.

"And here," Rudyard said. "You can have my lucky rock, too."

Everard's mouth fell wide open. "But what'll *you* do?" he said.

"I'll manage," Rudyard said, and pushed the rock toward him. "In case we don't see each other again," he said.

Everard held the rock up to the light. "You think we won't?"

"You can't never tell."

Everard dug down deep into *his* pocket, too. "Then, here," he said, and passed Rudyard something.

"What is it?" Rudyard asked.

"A cow tooth."

"*Oh, boy!*" Rudyard said. "It's just what I always wanted!"

"Well . . ." Everard said, as if he hesitated to make such a boast. "*Maybe* it's from a moose."

"A *moose* tooth!" Rudyard was overwhelmed. He was only sorry he had thrown away his petrified eyeball, or he would have given that to Everard, too.

Trim's store closed, then, and the men came out into the night, laughing and clearing their throats. Everything stopped, and the night was still. The boys listened till the men had gone. Then everything started up and the night began to work around the moon again. The loons and the seals and the sea ducks all began to talk at once. A cricket in the pilings tuned up while the wind scattered the phosphorescent sea like petals in the moonlight.

"You know where you ought to go?" Rudyard said, hoping to make Everard feel better.

"Where?" Everard said.

"Except it's the wrong way if you plan to stow away on the mailboat."

"*Where?*" Everard said again.

"Spain."

"What do I want to go there for?" Everard asked.

"Parpy went to Spain once. And he said the Portuguese are the best fishermen in the world, and he drank wine with them." Rudyard leaned a little closer. "You want to know what else?"

"What?"

Rudyard held back.

"*Tell* me," Everard said.

99

Rudyard straightened. "I drank wine once."

Everard perked up. "With who?"

"Parpy."

"You *did?*" Everard said. "How was it?" He leaned over so close that he could smell Rudyard's breath.

"It wasn't bad," Rudyard said, modestly. He hung his head. "Of course, I didn't get drunk."

"Oh," Everard said, no longer impressed.

They grew quiet for awhile, and then Everard said, "You sure you don't want to go, *too?*"

Rudyard considered. "Not if you're just going to join the army," he said "What else have you thought about?" He hadn't thought about much, himself, except becoming a gypsy.

"We could join the Masons," Everard said.

"Naw." Rudyard shook his head. "There ain't much I wanted to be except maybe a sea captain, and then a gypsy. Once I wanted to be a pirate."

"It's true about gypsies and pirates and all that stuff," Everard said. "They're all gone." He stopped before he went on, as if trying to think of something appealing. "All that's left is . . ."

Suddenly Everard was excited. "There *is* one thing," he said.

"What's that?"

"We could join the hippies!"

Rudyard looked up. "Why didn't *I* think of that?" he said. "*That* sounds like fun!"

"Yeah," Everard said, squatting on his haunches—"Mama don't like hippies."

"How come?"

"She said all they do is sing that loud music all day long, and they don't never take baths."

"*Never?*" Rudyard asked.

"According to Mama."

Rudyard was ready to leave immediately. "Where do we go to be hippies?"

"San Francisco," Everard said, as if *everybody* should know that. He had forgotten that Rudyard didn't have any television.

"And you know what else?" Everard asked.

"No," Rudyard said, "What?"

"We won't need any shoes, either."

"Why's that?"

"Hippies don't wear any."

"Oh," Rudyard said.

"Mama says that's why they got signs in restaurants: No Bare Feet Allowed. It's to keep the hippies out."

"Who wants to eat in a restaurant, *anyway?*" Rudyard said.

They had lots to talk about. They crawled out from under the wharf and walked along the shore. They took their time, scouring their feet in the wet sand below the high water mark. They stopped for awhile to listen. You can hear anything you want to hear in the surf. The waves rolling at Rudyard's feet whispered secrets of the universe. The tide ebbed away and left a long, shaggy mound of brown seaweed humped up along the rocks. In the tricky moon-light it looked like a sea monster. They watched it for a long time, then climbed the bank and walked up the road. Every light on the Nubble had been turned off, it was so late. The houses in the shadows were like veiled faces looking out at them as the boys passed.

The moon as it rose had turned pale white, shining now

through the clouds like a flashlight searching for tomorrow. Half-way up the road the boys heard a fox bark softly in the night. They stopped before the cemetery woods, to listen. When they reached the middle of the woods they stopped again and looked back at the church, behind them, where it stood like a monument to the dead.

It was awhile before Rudyard spoke. "On a full moon the rooster crows all night," he said. "The birds sing all night on a full moon, too. And . . ."

"*Hark!*" Everard said.

Rudyard drew in his breath.

"*Shhhh!*" Everard said. He meant it. "I *heard* something!"

But it was only the wind that came, rattling like the breath in a dead man's throat. The two boys moved closer, as if they were sheltering each other from it. Ahead and behind them, the black road was crawling with shadows.

Rudyard didn't hear anything except the wind, so, after awhile, "You know what?" he said, speaking so low that Everard could hardly hear him.

"What?"

"I think it was on a full moon when Satan stopped Parpy."

"Where?" Everard said.

"Over there," Rudyard said, pointing to the graveyard. "He came out from behind that hill—hoary eyed and resuscitating fire, Parpy said. He challenged Parpy to a game of solitaire."

Everard didn't say a word, but Rudyard could hear him swallow. After awhile Everard said, "I'm going home."

"Ain't we going to run away?"

"Not tonight."

"How come?"

"I changed my mind." Everard said.

"You changed it awful quick," Rudyard said. "How come?"

"We've got to grow some hair, first," Everard said, and measured—"down to here."

"How come you didn't think of that before?"

"I *did*," Everard said, trying to keep his voice to a whisper. "But I forgot."

"I think you're scairt," Rudyard accused.

"Of what?"

But Rudyard never got the chance to answer. "*Shhh!*" he said, and held his breath. Off to the side of the road, in the dark bushes that crouched there, something moved. Both boys turned as pale as the moon.

"I told you," Everard said, in a shaky little voice that fell out of his mouth like crumbs.

"Oh, *wait*!" Rudyard jumped. "Where you going?"

"Home." Everard turned.

"Oh," Rudyard said.

"Goodnight."

"See you."

"Me, too," Everard said.

They broke away slowly, each one holding the other with his eyes. The bushes all around them lurked. There they stood, waiting to see who would make the first move. Neither of them would.

Suddenly the bushes flew apart and the white thing lunged through the night toward them. Everard spun around and ground

103

his heels in for the take-off. Rudyard spun, too. Both boys knew they were on their own. They both headed home in different directions.

Rudyard ran so fast the wind made him bleary-eyed. It flapped in his hair like bat wings, playing in his ears insanely, like an orchestra. There wasn't time to look back. He looked up at the sky, chanting for the life of him, "I wish . . . I wish . . . I wish . . . I *wish* . . ." as if he had seen a falling star. But he couldn't think of one single wish that could save him from the terror that he heard, snorting behind him, galloping on Satan's hoofs. He wanted to holler, "I don't know *how* to play solitaire!" But when he opened his mouth, nothing would come out. His legs were churning up the road as if his feet were numb—and pretty soon they were.

When Rudyard reached home he was flying. He landed with both feet on the porch, head first, grabbing for the door. As he backed through he looked around. Marmy would know what to do for sure if it was Satan. But all he saw come bounding after him was Buttercups. She slowed down in the yard, her steps mincing. Her ears were stiff as a bat's in the night; her eyes were glowing in the moonlight.

Rudyard looked back behind her, expecting to see something more. But there was nothing. Up on the barn, the black-horse weathervane was creaking; on the door a slime-gray slug oozed across the screen. Rudyard shut the door and heaved himself against it. He stopped to listen to his heart. Its beating almost filled the house. It's a wonder that it didn't wake everybody up.

Rudyard straddled the stairs by threes, that night. He un-

dressed anxiously and crawled into bed with his moose tooth
clutched tightly in his fist. That night he said his prayers and
mumbled as he fell asleep, "I wish there was still gypsies."

-3-

Deep in sleep, Rudyard dreamed that he could fly. For awhile
he was the bird whose job it is every morning to greet the rising
sun. But one morning when the sun didn't rise, Rudyard flew
Away in search of it—out over the gray and frothing sea, until he
came to the mountains. Beyond the mountains he saw a rainbow;
and below the rainbow he saw a garden where watermelons grew,
sparkling under a ruby dew, and two-humped camels were strung
together with pearls. Rudyard flew down and landed on a path
beside a river and looked around. He hopped through the wonderful garden, admiring the flowers and the many tempting fruits
that hung from every limb.

The old man, when Rudyard came upon him sowing seeds,
introduced himself as the Gardener. He said that the sun wasn't
due to shine for a few days, and during that time, if Rudyard
liked, he could stay in the garden and be the Keeper of the Rainbow. There was only one condition: As long as he lived in the
garden, he must never taste any of its fruit.

Rudyard hadn't been hungry until the Gardener mentioned
the fruit. But after the old man disappeared, he felt starved.
Then, from high above his head, the purplest and juiciest plum
plopped handsomely at his feet. The plum was ripe, and Rudyard
reasoned that the Gardener only meant for him not to eat any of

the fruit while it still hung from the trees.

No sooner had Rudyard pecked the fruit than all his feathers tumbled out and he was turned to stone—a dumb rock, not even a lucky one. When the Gardener came back again he just picked up the rock and flung it into the river that swelled with cool, clear water sparkling like wine.

It took the water ages to wash the rock away, one particle at a time. But ages in a dream fleet by, and Rudyard suddenly found himself transformed and deposited in the sea. This time he was a boy, which was all right—except he was a boy without a name; and he had gills, which made him feel a little strange. He lived at the bottom of the sea, where he ate fish and burned dragons in his fire. He could have stayed forever, but when the sea learned that he didn't have any name, it was angered. It drove him away, out into the world to find one.

The boy without a name wandered for miles before he came to a town. He thought if he inquired around that he would find someone who would tell him which way he should go to get back to the wonderful garden. But when he looked, he found that all the houses had been built with no doors on which to knock and no windows to let in the light.

It was night when the boy came to the graveyard. He hurried to pass through but, before he could, the ground opened and out stepped Satan—hoary-eyed and resuscitating fire. Right then, when Rudyard needed them the most, he discovered that he had wings. He spread them wider as they grew, flapping as he flew— higher and higher. Until he flew away—out over the treetops and the rooftops and the chimney pots and the telephone-light poles

107

where birds were perched at the risk of being electrocuted. Rudyard flew out over sailboats on the sea.

Aunt Lucy saw him. She didn't know whether to be surprised that he could fly or mortified because he was free. Every time she spoke, moths came fluttering from her lips. She stood out on the end of Gooseberry Nubble, with her hands on her hips, and the wind that was clawing at her hair blew away the moths in a funnel.

Rudyard was disappointed when he opened his eyes and found himself back in the room where he had started. Out past the garret window he could see the cold fog creeping from the dawn. Down in the parlor he could hear Parpy twiddling the dial on his radio. When it came to WRKD, the voice of coastal Maine boomed up through the floor boards—*clear and warmer today with lots of sunshine*. The birds were celebrating in the trees. He could hear Marmy clattering the stove covers in the kitchen.

Rudyard loafed and yawned and took his time as if there was a plenty. He felt haunted, this morning, by the vague mystery of his dream, the memory of which had left him empty. He felt a little better when he came through the kitchen, and he got his appetite back completely when he heard Marmy in her pantry, knocking together a batch of fritter batter.

When Rudyard came out onto the porch, he was thinking— clam fritters, probably; or else zucchini; or maybe blueberry with honey. And thinking, too, about how sore his toes were, burning in the cold dew, Rudyard looked up. It was his habit. He never really expected to see Kite, perched there in the clear blue, unveiled by the mist and peeking down through the locust limbs. But there she was, waiting for him to bring her breakfast.

Rudyard seemed to behold a resurrection. He slapped himself. He started hollering, "Kite's back! *Kite's* back!" And before he knew what he was going to do, he spun around and stubbed his toe and banged through the screen door. In the parlor he mauled through Parpy's netting gear, strewing things across the floor.

"Here! Here!" Parpy said. "What're you *up* to?"

And Marmy stood above him, hugging her mixing bowl. "Land sakes alive, Plum. I should say as much. What's got *into* you?"

To Rudyard it almost seemed as if he had practiced for just such an emergency. He reeled a dozen arm-lengths of twine off a spool, and almost cut himself with the scissors. There wasn't time to explain things, now!

On his way through the kitchen, Rudyard reached around the corner to the pantry and grabbed a cold fish from the sink. He leaped through the door, off the porch. He ran, waving his fish at the sky. Before Kite could fly down to get it, he was halfway up the ladder. He climbed with his neck craned while he kept both eyes on his bird. She danced to see him coming. She sang for him—a hoarse, old sandy song.

"*Kite!*" Rudyard exclaimed, as he crawled through the little door. Kite thrust her beak into the fish and grabbed it from him.

Rudyard held onto the bird's leg as he worked—*quickly*. A single fish would distract her only for a second. He looped the twine and tucked it twice. He pulled it tight and tied a bowline on a bite, just the way Parpy had showed him. And there, where a nail stuck up, he wound the loose end of the string—around and

109

around and again—before he fastened it to the tower. He breathed deep, as if he had secured his fate.

The first thing Kite saw, when she had swallowed the fish, was that there weren't any more where that one had come from. *"Grawwk!"* she said. She arched her wings and coiled back her slender neck. She tilted off the tower's rim, trusting herself gracefully to the wind. It tickled Rudyard on the inside, and made him feel a little as if he were about to fly away, too. But when Kite reached the end of the string she snagged and went crashing in a tailspin.

Rudyard hurried to the tower's rim. He balanced on his toes and bent his nose out over it and looked down. Kite flounced around at the end of the string like a hen with her head cut off. She clawed and splintered the wood with her wings and knocked her head among the beams until Rudyard thought she would spill her brains out. He didn't know what to do, as she climbed— whether he should pull her in like a fish, or whether—he felt for his knife—he should cut her loose! But he didn't even have time to unfold his blade before Kite reached the top. She grabbed hold of the rim with her claws, and with her beak.

Rudyard watched Kite bite herself in her attempts to climb in. He could have helped her, but instead he stepped back out of her reach. He had a sudden, dreadful feeling about what Kite would do to him as soon as she knew what he had done to her. But she only ruffled up her feathers and shook her wings. The wind fluffed the feathers up along her neck, so that when she looked at him, with her fierce eyes glowing, she seemed to be wearing a war bonnet, behind the beak which was more accurate than a tomahawk.

Rudyard flinched.

Kite tried again. She flew in a circle, around and around, as if she had been hooked up to a carousel; her tail was a rudder, around and around; the world was blue, around and around and around—while Rudyard followed her. He imagined he flew, too —until he fell down, while the world continued. Rudyard tried to stand up, but he couldn't get his legs unwound. Everything was dizzy.

chapter five

Summer burned like a candle and the days fell away one by one like hot tallow drops—until September came. The days began to shorten, then; the nights grew long and cool; in the trees the wind was whispering of fall. Already the leaves began to change. The sumac leaves turned bright red, drooping on their stems like the plumage of a bird; the moosewood leaves were yellow tinged, like small, tanned pelts; and golden poplars spangled in the wind.

There were only three more days before school was to begin when Rudyard learned that it wouldn't begin yet, for another whole month. There was a new teacher coming from Away. Rudyard was glad for the delay. For one thing, it meant that Parpy would postpone giving him his school haircut. The way Rudyard figured it, a whole extra month would give his hair *plenty* of time to grow—while he was waiting for Everard to come and run away

113

with him to San Francisco.

Meantime, Rudyard stayed up in the tower and watched Uncle Harvey's lobster boat as it went, puttering on its course around the island. He had even smuggled into the tower Parpy's best pair of binoculars, which he could adjust to bring the boat right up close. He could see Uncle Harvey tending the winch and bossing Everard around, every time they hauled a trap and it was time to pick out the lobsters.

When Rudyard wasn't looking through the binoculars he was spending a lot of time untangling the string from his bird. When he let the string out, Kite would spread her wings and ride to the end of it. The wind would catch and carry her about, tossing her left and right; or sometimes she would fly in a circle—but that flight always snarled the string around her feet and dragged her down till she was limping like a cripple. Sometimes she snagged and crashed headfirst into the tower, as if she had broken her wings.

It took Kite a week to recover from her first few crashes. After that the bird flew a little less and resigned herself a little more to the perch—where she strolled, around and around on the tower's rim. She looked down between her long, wading-bird legs as if the wind were a stream in which she stalked the good things swimming in its current. All that ever came by, though, were the flies. They landed on the warm, stinking wood between Kite's feet, squatting long enough for her to aim her beak and nail them. And so his bird lived—on the fish that Rudyard brought her, and on a few measly flies she caught herself.

When Rudyard climbed down from the tower he carried in his

hair the knots the wind had tied, and he was always thinking, when they were apart—perhaps he should let the bird go. But, no matter how much he thought about it, when he climbed back up into the tower he always changed his mind.

When Everard came, Rudyard decided, *then* he would let Kite go. He only wished that Everard would hurry up, because he was anxious himself to be gone. Everywhere he looked it seemed that someone was going somewhere—in sailboats and jet planes; the summer people were all leaving. Wherever it was summer they were going, while Rudyard stayed in the tower as if he were stranded.

Even the cat disappeared for parts unknown and left Rudyard disappointed. Parpy said it happened every year. Along toward this time, he said, when everything is fat and the hunting is good, lots of changes take place. Mother cats traipse off into the woods to train their kittens to survive—how to hypnotize birds and charm mice, Marmy said. The cat would return but the kittens—if Rudyard ever saw them again—would be wild.

It was about this time that migration began, and the birds began to descend in dark flocks, cast from the sky like nets. They covered the trees and the house and the barn, plastering the roof-peaks white with their droppings. Here and there and everywhere that Dingbat was pointing, Rudyard saw birds. The sun shone purple on the backs of the blackbirds strung like black pearls the length of Marmy's clothesline, and on their wings when they lit out across the meadow in their raucous search for fat grass-hoppers. In the garden the finches found the sunflowers Marmy had planted for them. They stripped the seeds out one by one and

116

left the empty heads hanging. The birds in the orchard came looking for worms that were buried deep in the sweet apples that lay
flavored by the ground. The birds in the woodpile came listening
for bugs that scurried around under the sour bark. In the rain
barrel the birds were drinking and taking quick baths—splashing
themselves with their wings and dribbling tiny beakfuls of water
upon their breasts. So many birds flew over the tower that Rudyard thought it was a wonder he didn't catch one in his hair. But
not one of them offered to land there. To Rudyard it almost
seemed as if he had thrown a rock into the center of every flock
that came near, for the birds in every flock—the instant they saw
him standing there with Kite—darted away like minnows.

Although Rudyard liked to spend most of his time in the tower,
he took time out every day to walk to Gooseberry Nubble. He
carried a pail to lug Marmy's corn water in, and he looked along
the way—beneath the telephone-light poles—to find how many
birds had been electrocuted by the humming wires. The first day
migration began he found one, kinked among the weeds. On the
third day of migration he found two more. He untangled them
and brought them home to Marmy, who kept a trowel handy for
digging bird graves. Because of Kite their deaths meant more to
Rudyard, as if his friendship with the great blue heron related
him to all birds. Marmy helped him bury them—three more birds
in the animal cemetery. With a solemn heart she pronounced
them—a catbird, a cowbird, and a wren.

Aunt Lucy reported that she had seen Rudyard throwing rocks
at the birds, and *then* bringing them home to bury. But Marmy
only stiffened up a little at that, and declared she'd never heard of

such a thing. She knew he hadn't been deliberately going around killing birds. What Marmy *didn't* know was that he *had* been throwing rocks—one or two—which he had aimed to *ping* the wires and sting the ears of anyone gossiping on the telephones. He had decided that it was the gossiping that heated the wires until they hummed, so it was the gossipers who were responsible for killing the birds. What Rudyard was doing was paying them back, one good *ping* for every bird he found dead. He wondered if Aunt Lucy had gotten *her* ears stung.

"I'm going to ask Aunt Lucy, sometime, how come she hates me so much," Rudyard said.

-2-

The birds had been migrating for about a week when Marmy called Rudyard down from the tower, one day. She wanted him to accompany her on a bird hunt.

Buttercups tagged along after Rudyard, with Dingbat panting in their tracks. But Marmy wasn't long in making a rule that all goats should be barred from bird hunts, because goats don't sneak so good. Rudyard apologized to Dingbat for shutting him in the barn, too, but he said it wouldn't be any fun for Buttercups to stay without *some* company. He told the dog to go lie down in the hay. Dingbat looked abused, but he went, and as soon as he turned, Rudyard closed the door and ran. When he caught up with Marmy, she was on her way, and whistling like a bird.

Migrations were about the most excitement Marmy ever saw. They sent her stepping around the house and through the woods

118

with Parpy's binoculars, listening to the birds sing as if she were at an opera. Each year Rudyard followed her, asking such things as:

"From where does the wind blow?

"Where does the tide go when it's out?

"Where does a caterpillar get its wings?

"Where do green aphids go when the spit they live in freezes on the stem?"

And finally, "What makes the birds sing?"—as he listened to what seemed to him to be flutes and fiddles and a zither.

Marmy braced herself with a fresh breath of air. "A free creature is happy just to be alive," she said, and resumed her tour.

Some of the birds they saw were coming from the Arctic Circle, Marmy said. Some were going south, to Florida, and some were going to Cuba. And some, like the warblers, were even on their way to the Tropics.

"Panama, Labrador, Manitoba," Marmy said, as she named some places where birds go. And she repeated, "Panama, Labrador, Manitoba," as if the names were charms.

Marmy pointed out birds that Rudyard had never dreamed existed, birds that Marmy said were pied-billed grebes and horned larks and redstarts and Baltimore orioles. There was a cuckoo, too, and a scarlet tanager, and an indigo bunting. Rudyard had wondered, "Where is Indigo?"

But Marmy told him, "Land sakes, Plum—it isn't a place. It's a color, like in the rainbow."

They were looking for another indigo bunting that Marmy heard when she spied a mockingbird. She forgot about her feet, she got so excited, and trotted all the way home to check her book. According to the book, it couldn't be—not a mockingbird, not "way down East" in Maine. But Marmy *vowed* it was a mockingbird, and hard to miss the way it had been mocking that indigo bunting.

According to the book they couldn't see a pink flamingo, either. But Marmy was so positive that she had seen a mockingbird that Rudyard decided to keep an eye out, anyway.

"What makes all the birds stop here?" Rudyard asked, for it had never *seemed* that the island was any place in particular.

"Lord," Marmy said, "they've been traveling for days and stopping along their way for food and rest. The island is only one of them places that's right in line with the Great Atlantic Flyway, which is like a highway in the sky for birds, Plum. The wind currents up there are *high velocity*," Marmy said.

It was the first time Rudyard had ever heard Marmy use a word like *that*.

"All a bird needs to do," she explained, "once it gets up so high, is just climb onto one of them wind currents and ride."

Rudyard could just picture a wind current, like a silver streamlined train filled with bird passengers, ploughing through the clouds. But that still didn't explain to him how the birds knew which current to choose, for the wind blows in all directions—and birds don't follow maps.

"According to the book," Marmy said, "a bird is guided by its instinct."

But that didn't help Rudyard much, either.

"Instinct is something stirring, way down deep, like another sense," Marmy said. "It tells them when it's time to move. Winter's coming."

Marmy had spoken straight to Rudyard's heart. Immediately he knew, and he could feel it. If he didn't move pretty fast he was liable to end up in a worse predicament than the birds. Marmy had already brought out the catalogue and measured his feet. Pretty soon school would be starting and he would be wearing new shoes. He had outgrown his old ones. Pretty soon he would be taking hot baths beside the fire, and Marmy would be scouring his neck.

As soon as Marmy mentioned her feet, Rudyard excused himself to go lug her some corn water, and on the way to have his own bird hunt—for ones that were dead. But he didn't get far. As soon as he freed his prisoners from the barn he deserted them and climbed back up into the tower where he could think. He wanted to be alone.

So that must be what he had. For the first time ever, he said it. "*In*stinct."

Rudyard looked up at his bird. "That's what *you've* got," he said. And he thought, perhaps it was what his parents both had.

What would Aunt Lucy say?

Perhaps if he ran away, after he got to Sabathday, he could just rely on his—Rudyard said it again—"*In*stinct."

chapter six

Rudyard's loneliness grew with the passing of the year. He didn't know *why* he was lonely—or for *whom*. He thought he could be lonely for his mother and father, if you can miss someone you can't remember having met, or, he thought he could be lonely for his best friend. As each day passed and Everard never came, Rudyard was beginning to wish that school had started at its usual time. At least, then, Aunt Lucy would have a *job* keeping them apart.

After Labor Day, Rudyard climbed up into the tower more often, to adjust his binoculars and to wonder—what would he do if Everard never showed up? Should he run away alone and be a hippie? Or should he stay? If he stayed, he wouldn't want to set Kite free. She would fly away and he would be the only one left. But if he stayed, he couldn't keep her, either. Marmy would never consent to living under the same roof with a great blue heron. And if he left Kite out all winter, surely she would freeze. Rudyard shuddered at the thought of having to bury her, along with the other birds, in the animal cemetery. Hers would be the next biggest grave to the horse.

Every day Rudyard scanned through the binoculars, flicking through the treetops, until he came up behind Uncle Harvey's lobster boat. He leaped ahead of the boat and studied it from stem to stern, watching Everard hard at work. The wake behind the boat churned out and faded in the blue until it disappeared like a jetstream. Rudyard looked for a sign that Everard would be coming—*any* sign. But, the more he looked, the more he was disappointed, for he never saw anything unusual.

Marmy called the sky "October blue" when the leaves began to fall. Autumn began its passing like a parade, with banners flying and colors flaring everywhere. The wind in the sugar maples sent the red leaves flying like sparks. The leaves from the silver maples shimmered and were driven like schools of fish. Trees which had donned hundred-tinted robes of gold and orange flung their leaves to the winds and stood bare, their naked limbs sketched against the sky like ink. All across the gold-colored ground and down the path to the crick the leaves lay, and in the naked limbs the abandoned birds' nests were exposed.

Rudyard counted seventeen of the nests, one day, on his way to the crick, each cradled in the crotch of a tree like a little basket. Some of them had been molded from sticks and mud daubings, and some of them had been woven from moss and shreds of leaves. Under a fallen mantle of leaves Rudyard searched and found the frail, blue-speckled bits of shell which were all that remained of an egg. He brought the big piece home, gently, in his fist to show to Marmy—marveling all the while. So *many* birds had hatched and grown to sing. And now they all were gone, leaving the air silent in their memory.

Rudyard wondered if the herons had gone, for they were always among the last to leave. He hadn't seen one in a long time. It made him sad to think of Kite's being the only bird left, except for those who stayed all winter. He tried hard to make it up to her by spending a lot of time with her and feeding her more fish than she could eat. He even offered to share the binoculars with her, but it was difficult for Kite, whose beak stuck out for a foot in front of her eyes. When she *did* get a peek she only shook her head and blinked.

With autumn came the frost, and after that the harvest—and not much time, any more, for Rudyard to play. The day the harvest began he lagged behind, but Marmy snapped him out of it by putting him in full command of the cellar. It was hard for Marmy to get down there, and Parpy said he wasn't as limber about ladders as *he* used to be, either.

During the harvest Rudyard was back and forth between the pantry and the cellar a dozen times a day, lugging the things that had to be stored for winter. Parpy came down as often as he could —to sample the crisp, dill pickles he had put up in a crock, and to sample the sauerkraut, too. Or sometimes he held his rhubarb wine up to the light to see that it wasn't clouding. Parpy liked his wine to sparkle as clear as the spring water from which he brewed it.

Parpy was pleased when he looked around and saw the good job

that Rudyard was doing in the cellar. One shelf was lined with crab apples stewed in honey, their pink faces pressed against the jars, looking out through bars of cinnamon. There were three shelves of spiced mackerel, half a dozen to a jar, floating in their own brine. Below the mackerel was a shelf lined with mincemeat, and the piccalilli made from green tomatoes. On the next shelf came the sweet pickles and the marmalade Marmy had made from the rind of their Fourth of July watermelon—and between the jars Rudyard had alternated rosehip jam and chokecherry jelly. Everything on *that* shelf was a favorite. He favored the red raspberry preserves, too, and the blueberry, and the blackberry, and the tiny jars of wild strawberry, their thick juices beaded up and seeping out around the wax seals like honey. The preserves, in all, took up five whole shelves, counting, in between, one long row of apple butter. That completed one wall in the cellar.

On another wall Rudyard had lined the shelves with nineteen one-pint jars of pickled beets, three one-gallon jars of pickled eggs, and a quart of rhubarb sauce for every week right up until the first of May. There were dandelion and beet greens, and corn on the cob, and somewhere—stewed tomatoes, which Rudyard had stashed in behind, as if he didn't want to remind anybody.

Being in full charge of the cellar didn't turn out to be nearly as bad as Rudyard had figured, for toward the end Marmy began to stock her pantry for the winter with a special order from Trim's store. Every time he passed through the pantry, on his way to the cellar, he took a whiff to tickle his palate. When the time came to harvest apples, Rudyard struggled with each thundering bucketful, stopping in the pantry often to gather his strength. He filled

the cellar bins with russets and wolf rivers and dark red baldwins
—apples to fry and bake, and some to make sauces and pies and
upside-down apple cake. He filled a bin full of Aroostook potatoes, too, as soon as Parpy had dug them and they were dry. By
that time Rudyard had found the chocolate bits in Marmy's pantry, and dark corners that were stuffed with dates and nuts. He
knew of shelves behind closed doors where secrets were kept high
up with only their odors to hint—cinnamon and nutmeg and ginger, and cardamon seeds Marmy crushed for the frosted yeast rolls
she made just right to come undone inside someone's mouth.

Even while Rudyard was helping braid the onions he thought
of Marmy's pantry. And after he lugged the onions down and
hung them up in the cellar in golden bunches that ranged the
whole length of two floor beams, Marmy's pantry was still on his
mind. Its odors enticed him, even though the cellar itself was a
nice place to be now that the cold, fragrant apples filled the bins.

After almost a week of steady work there were only a few things
left for Rudyard to do in the cellar. He polished the sugar pumpkins and lined them up for pies and puddings. He lined up the
butternut squashes, too, making them ready to be clam-stuffed
and baked, along with the goat cheese that was mellowing. The
wooden boxes on the floor Rudyard filled with sand and packed
with beets and carrots. And anywhere there was room, he lined up
the rutabagas and the heads of cabbage.

The last thing that was left in the garden was the seed cucumber, a ripe yellow one that glowed in the sun among the grasses
and the frost-burned vines. Parpy picked it, and on his way in he
polished it on his felt pants—anticipating the next year's cucum-

ber patch. He placed it in the south window in the kitchen, beside the green tomatoes that were lined up there to ripen.

The cranberries were the last thing Marmy harvested. She took her bucket to the bog one day and filled it with the wax-red nuggets that had been nipped just right by the frost. She brought enough home for sauce and some to be strung for Christmas decorations. She and Rudyard spread them out on a sheet, in the garret, beneath the hanging sweet herbs. Marmy said that did her up good for the year. Marmy marked her yearly "retirement" by the harvest. Now all she wanted was to stay close by the fire and knit mittens. It was up to Rudyard, she said, to keep the woodbox full and to lug out the ashes.

Rudyard was kept so busy getting ready for winter that he almost forgot about being lonely. And he didn't think so much about Everard any more, either. Occasionally he felt the back of his neck. As his hair grew, it started to tickle his spine, and Rudyard knew—if Everard *did* come, he was ready.

-2-

The summer people were mostly gone by the time Marmy retired. And since Parpy was left with no place to peddle his fish, he decided to haul the net for the last time and retire, too. He had been expecting the mackerel to stop running, anyway, for more than a week. He said, at least they should be slacking off. But that afternoon, when he and Rudyard rowed the boat out into the cove, they were surprised. All along the net's floats the silver fish boiled up, slapping their tails on the surface of the water.

As they hauled the net aboard it was Rudyard's job to unsnarl the gills and pick out the fish from the twine web, while Parpy swung an oar and swore at a seal that never should have come so close. After awhile Rudyard was wading in live fish, which were gasping and wriggling around his bare feet, and he and Parpy were covered in scales that glittered like distant windows in the sunset.

They mounded the wet net in the stern when they were done and headed home. That end of the boat was weighed down so low that Rudyard had to perch in the bow to balance things out while Parpy rowed. The *Patient Lucy* plodded through the waves like a plowhorse. When Rudyard looked up, the sun was no longer shining brightly in the treetops, as it usually was when they had caught their share. The red sky faded to gray. Soon the dusk would begin to fill the air. The fish were grimacing, stiff, and Rudyard felt the cold begin to fill his feet.

They were almost ashore before Rudyard noticed the bird standing beneath the bank. It was so still that Rudyard thought, at first, he had created it—until it raised one leg. From the heron's foot the water fell in drops, like hot mercury, splashing in a silver ring that widened before Rudyard's eyes, leaving him spellbound. The heron raised its head, and, as they passed, its wings, unfolding them in silence. It overwhelmed Rudyard so that he stood straight up in the boat. Parpy stopped rowing and looked, with his oarfins dripping, while the heron disappeared, turning into the night.

When the dory came aground, Rudyard jumped out, thrilled by what he had seen. Parpy climbed over the side, sloshing in his hip boots. Together they hauled the boat ashore and silently

began the chore of unloading it—bailing the fish out in buckets and lugging them up the bank to the wheelbarrow. Rudyard worked fast to finish the job, and he was glad when it was done. He wanted to make it home in time to feed Kite, before it got too dark.

Parpy was glad when the fish were unloaded, too, for it was his last catch. He had been farming and fishing hard all summer, and now it was coming time to relax. Parpy fixed his thumbs behind his green suspenders and stepped back to look around. "Soon as the crows pick it clean, we can hang the net up in the barn," he said. "And when we get around to it, soon, we can upend the *Patient Lucy*." Parpy motioned toward the bank. He thumped Rudyard on the back, as if he were congratulating him.

But Rudyard didn't feel much like congratulations. And he didn't say much. He was satisfied that the mackerel season was over, too, but he was beginning to worry. After this, what was he going to feed Kite?

Parpy had built up the sides of his wheelbarrow extra high for just such a catch, but still the wheelbarrow was overflowing. The tree roots twisted out into the crooked path, making their passage difficult. Every time the wheelbarrow bumped, the fish on top of the slippery pile jiggled off and thumped to the ground as if it were made of solid rubber. It was Rudyard's job to pick the fish up and put it back, without knocking off another. He thought it would be easier for him if Parpy steered *around* the roots, so he asked. But there were so many roots, and all of them were so well hidden under the fallen leaves, that no matter how hard Parpy tried to miss them, it seemed as if he hit every one. Rudyard was having a trial going after the fish and at the same time keeping up, his shorter legs and bare feet scuffling through the leaves beside Parpy who was striding along in hip boots.

Rudyard was glad when they stopped to rest. He took some time to look around at the autumn-colored mushrooms which had started growing by the path and disappeared into the somber woods, inviting his mind to wander. He tried not to worry about what he was going to feed Kite. Perhaps he could go fishing with his hand line and catch enough cunners to feed the bird—at least until Everard came.

"By Tophet!" Parpy said. "With the cellar so full, and no one to sell them to, it brings to mind but one thing we can do with this lovely mess of mackerel."

"What's *that*?" Rudyard asked.

"Trade 'em with Uncle Harvey for a hod of lobsters," Parpy said. But then he looked a little glum. "It's a shame to see good mackerel go for lobster bait, when redfish or herrin' or even smelts would do as good, and none of them so hard to come by. But *lobsters* . . ." He smacked his lips and changed his tune completely. "A hod of lobsters wouldn't be bad at all. With a hod of lobsters we could celebrate in style, with some of your grandmother's cooking." He winked at Rudyard. "And maybe even break out a bottle of wine."

"Oh, *boy*!" Rudyard said. "Will Marmy play the organ?"

"We can ask her," Parpy said.

"I want to hear 'The Beer Barrel Polka,' first," Rudyard said.

They both were in the mood.

Now that Rudyard knew he was on his way to a celebration, he

133

didn't have half the trouble keeping up when Parpy started on, although he hobbled along picking out a pantlegful of beggar lice. When they came through the alder swamp the wheelbarrow squeaked along smoothly over the path and Parpy talked about the time, years ago at low tide, when he had collected lobsters in wheelbarrows to feed the hogs.

In the meadow the frost had been light. It had turned green edges brown and brightened up the goldenrod and wild blue asters. As they drew near the house, Rudyard looked up and saw Marmy on the porch, resting in her rocking chair. And resting there beside her was Thankful.

Immediately Rudyard looked away, at the hens that were moving in a slow current toward the barn on their way to roost. When Buttercups saw Parpy coming she flicked her ears and pranced off toward the barn, too, where she would wait for him to wash his hands and milk her. It was past the time.

Dingbat ran out and sashayed all around them, with greetings. He wagged his tail and licked the salt from Rudyard's hands. And Marmy was glad to see them. "Home at last," she said. She sounded relieved. "What kept you?"

Parpy parked the wheelbarrow at the bottom of the steps so Marmy could see. "Glory be!" she said. "What'll we *do* with 'em all?"

"We've already decided," Parpy told her. "We're going to trade with Harvey for a hod of lobsters. Tonight we're going to have us a long-overdue celebration."

Marmy liked celebrations, especially long-overdue ones. "What'll we celebrate *this* time?" she asked.

"*Life!* The same as we celebrated all the other times!" Parpy said. "It's that time of year. All that's left for us to do is buckle on the storm windows and chop wood."

"Land sakes!" Marmy said, as if she had forgotten to wind her watch. "It *is* that time. I'll have to bake a pie!"

"Oh, boy!" Rudyard said. "*Strawberry rhubarb!*"

Thankful's eyes bugged out at just the mention of a celebration. But she and Rudyard both knew that Aunt Lucy would never let her come.

'Will you play the organ at our celebration?" Rudyard asked.

"You-bet-I-will, Plum," Marmy promised, and tapped her toe. "Though you'll be the one who'll have to *pump!*"

Thankful snickered.

"What's the matter with *her*?" Rudyard asked.

Thankful snickered again. "Whoever heard of a boy called Plum?" she said. And then she sneered, the way she'd seen Aunt Lucy do.

Rudyard could feel his hair begin to stand straight up. But just then Aunt Lucy stalked into the yard, stinging the air with a switch. "I thought I told you to be home *before* it started to get dark," she said, addressing Thankful. "*Well?* Don't you think it's started?"

Thankful had already picked one fight, and Rudyard was just limbering up. The sight of Aunt Lucy standing before him made his blood rush. It must have showed.

Aunt Lucy silenced her switch. "Well," she said again. "What's the matter with *you*?" She turned her bony face toward Rudyard. It was a face like one Rudyard had seen in a picture of a totem

135

pole, with a chin that stuck way out, like an elbow.

"Nothing's the matter with *me*," Rudyard said. And, since he had been meaning to ask, he added, "What's the matter with *you*?"

That was all it took.

"Did you hear *that*?" Aunt Lucy said. She completely forgot about Thankful. When Rudyard looked, Thankful was thumbing her nose at him.

"Did I hear what?" Marmy asked.

Aunt Lucy smirked. "Filled with sarse, is he?" She turned to Rudyard, deliberately twitching her switch.

Rudyard stood his ground, glaring back at Aunt Lucy's scalding eyes. He flinched only once, when he glanced down and saw the veins crawling out like worms on Aunt Lucy's neck. He hadn't seen her *this* mad since the time she caught him and Everard playing cards on Sunday. "If you ain't *just like* your mother . . ." Aunt Lucy accused.

"Now, now," Marmy said, trying to keep the peace. Marmy never spoke much when Aunt Lucy was around.

"Now don't you go stickin' up for him," Aunt Lucy said. "He's a treacherous little sneak, he is—from the word *go*!"

But nobody needed to stick up for Rudyard. "I can stick up for myself," he said. "And I ain't no sneak!"

"*Huh!*" Aunt Lucy said, addressing Marmy as her mediator. "Listen to him, will you?" But then she turned to Rudyard. "As if I didn't know about the night you and Everard snuck out. . . . As if I didn't know about *all* the escapades you two got up your sleeves. Well, I can tell you now, *give up*! Everard got a good

lickin' for that night. And it's time you got one, too!" She stepped toward him. "There's nothin' would do you better than to
be taken down a peg or two!"

"Now, now," Parpy interfered. He planted a hip boot between
them. "If there's any licking to be done . . ." He fixed a hard eye
on Aunt Lucy.

Aunt Lucy was horrified. She backed away, but as soon as she
was a few feet from Parpy she turned on him, narrowing her eyes
and humping her back like a cat. Aunt Lucy was bristling. "*You*
take the side of that despicable little brat," she said. "He's your
little *Plum*, you say. You uphold him in everything he does, and
every day he gets a little bolder. Turn him over to the state, I told
you! Isn't that what I said? *They* know what to do with such cases!
There's no glory in raising someone else's illegitimate brat!"

Marmy stood straight up out of her chair.

"Ill-e-*gitimate*!" Aunt Lucy said. "I'm here to say it whether
you like it or not. You'll look back and rue the day you took that
brat in hand!" Aunt Lucy was so filled with her own bitterness
that she looked as if she had bitten down on a slug.

Rudyard was wondering what Aunt Lucy meant, but she didn't
give him the chance to ask. "It means you haven't got any father,"
Aunt Lucy said, "in case you've been doing any wondering. And
worse than that, it means you never *had* one!" Aunt Lucy lowered
her tone and drew her face in a little closer to Rudyard's own. "So
you see," she said, "there isn't any need of you going around actin'
so high and mighty. When you was born your mother couldn't
show her face in this town for a year. And when she did they put
her to scorn and drove her out."

Aunt Lucy sounded triumphant. "You want to hear all about your mother, don't you? You want to hear all about how she nastied up our name and how she ran away to hide her shame when she couldn't stand it any more, don't you? Why," Aunt Lucy huffed, "that mother of yours created a scandal big enough for this town to grow on for the next forty years!" Aunt Lucy lost control of her voice, then, and all her words went out of range.

That was when Parpy stepped in and shook Aunt Lucy by her shoulders. "You've said it all," he said.

And before Rudyard knew it, Marmy was down off the porch— hanging onto Parpy's arm. "Remember your heart, John."

Aunt Lucy opened her mouth to speak, but nothing more came out. Rudyard had seen a dog once, acting the same way—when it had a bone caught in its throat. Aunt Lucy whirled toward the porch. *"Thankful!"* she barked, and grabbed Thankful by a wrist.

Thankful stumbled to her feet. Aunt Lucy towed her out of the yard by leaps, so fast that Rudyard thought his cousin's arm was going to be yanked right out of its socket.

They were almost out of sight when Parpy hollered. His voice was touched with spite. "You tell Harvey to save out a hod of lobsters for tonight. You tell him I said I'm coming to get them. We're going to *celebrate!*"

-3-

Rudyard had a lot of questions he wanted to ask, but he couldn't word any of them. He and Parpy stood there, both looking at Marmy—or at the slippers on her knobby feet. Marmy

138

climbed the porch steps and sat down. She leaned back in her chair and felt inside her apron pocket for a tea leaf to chew, or a piece of cracked corn to relieve the tension. After awhile Marmy confirmed, "So we're going to have a celebration."

Marmy seemed to grow conscious of something missing, and she looked down at the shadow of the armchair as evening drew it taut across her empty lap. This was the time of day when Hey-Diddle-Diddle should be sleeping there, but the cat was still off somewhere with her kittens, teaching them how to hunt. Marmy's rockers tattered the silence.

"Talking about this, that, and the other," Marmy said—Marmy looked distraught, changing the subject. "After all, I miss my ratter, but I hope she doesn't come home before six weeks is up. Your grandfather says if she does it's a sure sign of a hurricane a coming. And the almanac this year predicts a whopper."

Marmy breathed deep. "It's that time of year," she said. "We'll have to keep an eye out—keep an eye out for the hurricanes, first, and keep an eye out for the mailboat, too. It should be bringing that new teacher any day, now. And your new shoes, Plum. I don't know *what* ails that catalogue. Them shoes should have come weeks ago."

But no matter *how* much Marmy talked, Rudyard had made up his mind not to forget what Aunt Lucy had called him. "Maybe the hurricane will blow the school *away*," he said.

It took Marmy by surprise. She raised her brow, "*Then* what would you do?"

"Lately I been thinking," Rudyard said, "with so many people leaving, maybe I'll be one of them."

139

"Leaving?" Marmy said. "What kind of talk is that to make?"

Rudyard shook his head. They might as well know.

"Without an education?" Marmy asked. "What will become of you?"

"Perhaps I'll be a hippie."

"A *hippie!*" She didn't believe him. "Land sakes, Plum! We ain't turned out with a hippie in the family, have we? What would Aunt Lucy say?"

"Wait till she finds out!" Rudyard boasted. "Everard might be one, too."

"*Two* hippies in the family!" Marmy chuckled. "Look what's become of us!"

But Parpy took him more seriously. "There's more you ought to know before you go traipsing off into the world to become a hippie," Parpy said. "The radio is *full* of hippies—and all this pollution and revolution and all them politicians palavering over what they're gonna do so long as the people keep flocking 'em over the money to do it with."

Marmy disapproved of the way Parpy was working himself up, and soon as she saw her chance she leaned forward in her chair. "You know what's going to happen?" Marmy snapped. She pointed at the sky, which was her way, Marmy said, of fitting a word in edgewise.

Rudyard could hardly wait to ask, "What?"

Marmy bugged her eyes out. "The *end* of the world!"

Rudyard looked from her to Parpy. When Parpy frowned, he had a chain of mountains in his forehead.

"*But,*" Marmy rejoiced, fitting another word in edgewise,

"there'll be salvation. Everybody wants to be saved!"

Marmy heisted herself up out of the chair, brushing her lap as if it were full of cat hairs. She breathed deep, filling up her big bosom. She looked at them both. "Tonight the smell of ripe apples is in the air, and the crickets are fiddling in the cattails." She let her breath out. "Just the night for a celebration," Marmy said, "and though I could sit here forever, it's time for me to go, now, and tend to supper." She turned abruptly and hurried inside.

Rudyard was anxious to leave, too, but he knew by the way Marmy had acted that Parpy still had something to say. "I wonder if you understand," Parpy said. "You're old enough." He laid a hand on Rudyard's shoulder.

Rudyard pulled away. Even though Parpy had stuck up for him, he was still filled with resentment. "Does Aunt Lucy under-stand?" Rudyard asked.

Parpy was silent.

"Well?" Rudyard demanded. "*Does* she?"

"No," Parpy said. "That's just the trouble. Aunt Lucy *doesn't* understand."

Rudyard looked up at his bird. Some of Kite's feathers had fallen down one by one, around the tower, like petals falling around a vase of flowers. "I've got to go feed Kite, now," he said, "before it gets any darker." He stepped up to the wheelbarrow and took a pair of mackerel in each hand.

Parpy let him go without another word.

142

Rudyard's hands were full of fish as he climbed, hugging the ladder. When he reached the top he crawled in through the door and stood up. He didn't even think about feeding his bird. He didn't even look around. His mind was someplace else. Kite just bent over him and grabbed the fish, one at a time, and devoured them.

Rudyard wiped both hands across his jeans and dug down deep into his pocket. He took his moose tooth out, absent mindedly, and began to polish it. Aunt Lucy had said a lot, and left Rudyard's thoughts as tangled as his yellow hair. He tried to figure it out about his mother. Maybe she had gotten where she was going, wherever she had gone—or maybe she had gotten lost.

"Instinct," Rudyard said, and looked up at his bird.

He tried to figure it out about his father, too. He felt as he had felt when he heard there weren't any more sea captains left—or gypsies, either. And he repeated, "Ill-e-gitimate." Now he knew why Aunt Lucy hated him, and probably always would, until the day he died. And that was why Everard was never coming. Rudyard gave his moose tooth one last look, for luck, and stuffed it way back down into his pocket.

When Rudyard brought his knife out, unfolding the blade, he wasn't sure *what* he was going to do. He was half stunned, looking at Kite and at the string that blew so carelessly in his direction. Kite was becoming such a bedraggled bird. Rudyard thought of the magnificent heron that he and Parpy had seen, standing on the rim of the shore. Its wings in flight had whispered like the waves to the air. There had been magic in the bird. What would Marmy say it meant? And how could he be sure? In a world where omens, even, don't come true, how could he be sure of *any*thing?

It happened so quickly, and it was so simply done that when the string was cut Kite never moved, but sat there, dumbly glowering. Rudyard had to act before he changed his mind.

"Go on!" he said. "*Git!*" He hated to drive her.

Kite shrugged her wings and coiled back her slender neck. "Don't you know?" Rudyard cried. "You're free!" And so saying, he stepped in quickly and bunted Kite up under her breast.

Kite grabbed at him and missed as she went sailing off. She caught the wind to fly in a circle . . . and around she flew . . . barely stirring the air with her great wings. But she came back to the rim of the tower as if she were still tied.

"You're *free!*" Rudyard hollered, jumping up and down. He waved his fists before Kite's eyes, as if trying to wake her. "You're *free!* You're *free!*"

Kite was not afraid of him. She blinked and leaned with little concern, and caught the wind to fly in a circle . . . effortlessly riding on her wings . . . around and around. Rudyard turned with her until he was dizzy. When she broke the circle, it took his breath away.

Kite looked back only once before she flew up high, climbing in the sky on wings that opened wide and wider. When she saw that she was free she just kept right on going, straight out over the dark treetops and over the sea, until she was only a silhouette. Each stroke of her wings swelled in his throat as Rudyard watched.

144

Marmy said it was bad luck to watch a good friend go out of sight. Rudyard let the hand he had raised as if to wave drop uselessly at his side. He looked down. All that was left him of his bird was a pile of droppings. His throat broke and spread through him in a terrible rush.

-5-

Awhile after Rudyard had stopped crying, he crawled out through the little door and onto the ledge of the tower. He waited for a long time, at the top of the ladder, staring away into the night. He began to wonder—where would Kite go in this world? If, like Marmy said, it was near the end, did that mean the end for birds, too? Was it possible for a bird to stay up so high in the sky that nothing could touch it? Could it fly forever, if it lived on bugs? So that even if there wasn't any world left it wouldn't bother the birds—*some* birds? He hoped it wouldn't bother Kite.

Slowly, from out of the lonely night sounds, something came to Rudyard. Something he remembered that he used to do, which he hadn't done in a long time. He closed his eyes and opened up his mind and flew—out over the treetops and the rooftops and the chimney pots and the telephone-light poles where the birds perched. He flew out over sailboats on the sea. Aunt Lucy saw him. She didn't know whether to be surprised that he could fly or mortified because he was free. Every time she spoke, the moths came fluttering from her lips. She stood out on the end of Gooseberry Nubble, with her hands on her hips, and the wind that was clawing at her hair blew away the moths in a funnel.

146

When Rudyard opened his eyes it was the same as waking from a dream. And at the same time, Marmy was calling him. When he looked down, Marmy had lit a lamp that sent out a beacon in the night for the moths that came to butt softly against the window.

Rudyard hesitated to go down, at first. That was before he thought—school would be starting in a few days. He would be seeing Everard, then, for sure.

Marmy called him again. "Come, Plum.

"Sup-perrr!" Marmy chimed.

And Rudyard knew. As soon as they ate he would help Marmy clean the plates, while Parpy stepped out to fetch the lobsters. By the time Parpy was home Marmy would be warming up the organ, while Rudyard pumped. Before they got to going *too* good, Parpy would go down cellar to select a new bottle of wine—or maybe Rudyard would be sent. Later on Parpy might even do the hy-biddy-woodchuck. That would be sometime around midnight, before the feast. Tomorrow they would all sleep late.

"*Yooo-hoooo!*" Marmy hollered.

The moon was glooming on the sea and the geese were migrating down from Canada in a sharp V. Rudyard backed into the ladder and started down.

ABOUT THE AUTHOR

DARRELL A. ROLERSON was born in 1946 on the island of Islesboro, in Maine, where he grew fond of the people who live there and experienced the things he most enjoys writing about. He remained on the island until he graduated from high school. For one year after leaving home he worked as a stenographer with a legal firm in Massachusetts. The next two years he spent in Washington, D.C., where he enlisted in the Navy. In 1968 and 1969 his first real ambition was fulfilled when he hitchhiked across country three times, enjoying himself between trips in San Francisco. In 1970, his first book, *A Boy and a Deer*, was published. This was followed by *Mr. Big Britches*, *In Sheep's Clothing*, and *A Boy Called Plum*.

Currently, the author alternates travel with life on Islesboro, pruning his apple trees, learning to keep honey bees, and discovering some interesting things about herbs. He says of himself, "I am a farmer, first, and only incidentally a writer."

ABOUT THE ARTIST

TED LEWIN was born in Buffalo, New York, and studied art at Pratt Institute, in Brooklyn. He supported himself while in school by wrestling professionally, and, upon graduation, he was the recipient of the Dean's Medal. Mr. Lewin is married, and he and his wife, who is an artist, too, live in Brooklyn.